"Aren't you happy?"

Caleb's question brought a lump to Whitney's throat. For a long time she had viewed herself as a woman who had it all—a luxurious apartment, a successful career, a fiancé pledging to share the future with her. But now Caleb was making her wonder if those things had actually fulfilled her.

"I—oh, Caleb," she said. "I don't know what it's like to be happy anymore."

Suddenly his hands were on her shoulders, drawing her to him. Whitney knew she should pull away, be strong and drag all her emotions back under control. But she wanted this man to hold her.

Caleb stroked her hair. "It's all right. Everyone feels alone and afraid sometime."

"It's more than that, Caleb. I—I've made a mess of things."

His finger moved beneath her chin and drew her face up to his. "I doubt that," he said with a seriousness that took her by surprise.

Whitney's gaze roamed over his face until it finally settled on his mouth. "You can't say that. You don't know me."

"No. But I'd like to."

Dear Reader,

Happy Spring! It's May, the flowers are blooming and love is in the air. It's the month for romance—both discovery and renewal—the month for mothers and the time of new birth. It's a wonderful time of year!

And in this special month, we have some treats in store for you. Silhouette Romance's DIAMOND JUBILEE is in full swing, and *Second Time Lucky* by Victoria Glenn is bound to help you get into the springtime spirit. Lovely heroine Lara discovers that sometimes love comes from unexpected sources when she meets up with handsome, enigmatic Miles. Don't miss this tender tale! Then, in June, *Cimarron Knight*, the first book in Pepper Adams's exciting new trilogy— *CIMARRON STORIES*—will be available. Set on the plains of Oklahoma, these three books are a true delight.

The DIAMOND JUBILEE—Silhouette Romance's tenth anniversary celebration—is our way of saying thanks to you, our readers. To symbolize the timelessness of love, as well as the modern gift of the tenth anniversary, we're presenting readers with a DIAMOND JUBILEE Silhouette Romance title each month, penned by one of your favorite Silhouette Romance authors. In the coming months writers such as Marie Ferrarella, Lucy Gordon, Dixie Browning, Phyllis Halldorson—to name just a few—are writing DIAMOND JUBILEE titles especially for you.

And that's not all! Laurie Paige has a heartwarming duo coming up—*Homeward Bound*. The first book, *A Season for Homecoming*, is coming your way in June. Peggy Webb also has *Venus de Molly*, a sequel to *Harvey's Missing*, due out in July. And much-loved Diana Palmer has some special treats in store during the months ahead....

I hope you'll enjoy this book and all of the stories to come. Come home to romance—Silhouette Romance—for always!

Sincerely,
Tara Hughes Gavin
Senior Editor

STELLA BAGWELL

That Southern Touch

Silhouette Romance

Published by Silhouette Books New York

America's Publisher of Contemporary Romance

To Mary and Tex,
my Toledo Bend friends...
on the Texas side

SILHOUETTE BOOKS
300 E. 42nd St., New York, N.Y. 10017

ISBN: 0-373-08723-3

First Silhouette Books printing May 1990

Books by Stella Bagwell

Silhouette Romance

Golden Glory #469
Moonlight Bandit #485
A Mist on the Mountain #510
Madeline's Song #543
The Outsider #560
The New Kid in Town #587
Cactus Rose #621
Hillbilly Heart #634
Teach Me #657
The White Night #674
No Horsing Around #699
That Southern Touch #723

STELLA BAGWELL

lives with her husband and teenage son in southeastern Oklahoma, where she says the weather is extreme and the people are friendly. When she isn't writing romances, she enjoys horseracing and touring the countryside on a motorcycle.

Stella is very proud to know that she can give joy to others through her books. And now, thanks to the Oklahoma Library for the Blind in Oklahoma City, she is able to reach an even bigger audience. The library has put her novels on cassette tapes so that blind people across the state can also enjoy them.

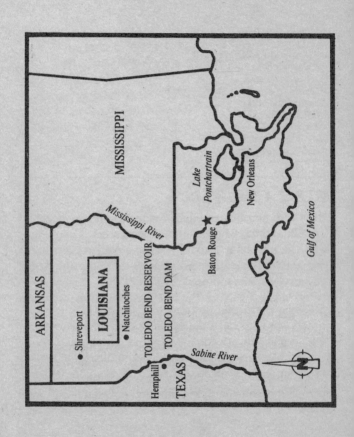

Chapter One

"Whitney Drake, this is total insanity," she spoke aloud. "What are you doing on this godforsaken back road in Louisiana?"

"Running," she answered herself grimly. Running to. Running from. Whitney hadn't figured that out yet. She did know, however, that this was not her night. Already she'd made two wrong turns and darkness had caught up to her before she could find a town large enough to have any kind of motel accommodations.

To make matters worse, rain was pelting against the car in waves of white sheets. The rapid swipe of the windshield wipers was fighting a losing battle against the downpour. At the most, visibility was only ten feet in front of the headlights. Yet even if Whitney could see, she wasn't quite certain she'd taken the right road this time.

To add to her doubts, asphalt suddenly gave way to dirt road. It was boggy from the rain and she felt her Jaguar sink as she hit the muddy surface. She slowed immediately, then decided to pull the car over to the side and stop. With the motor still running, she rolled down the window for a clearer look.

In front of her was dense forest. To the left and right was the same. Now that Whitney thought about it, several miles had passed since she'd even seen a house.

This is not a good sign, Whitney, she told herself. Not a good sign at all. A dirt road can only be leading you to a swamp, or Lord only knows what else.

A gust of wind blew in the window, bringing the cool sting of rain. Whitney quickly rolled up the window then reached to the passenger seat for a map.

She'd been traveling on Highway 84, then she'd made a left in order to merge with 71. So far she hadn't found 71 or the town of Natchitoches. But it was hardly her fault that there were so many side roads and unclear highway signs to confuse her.

Deciding a U-turn was the only way back to civilization, Whitney put the car into gear and pulled out onto the road again. The beam of the headlights lit the narrow mire of mud. She cursed under her breath as she realized there was not enough room for the turn without backing up.

Grateful that at least there was no traffic to worry about, she put the car into reverse. Slowly she eased backward. The going was fine for three feet, then the tires hit a deep rut and began to spin.

Even more frustrated, Whitney stepped down harder on the accelerator in an effort to dislodge the tires. After a moment the tires caught grip on drier ground and spun free. Before Whitney could ease her foot off the accelerator, the car shot backward.

She jammed on the brakes, but it was too late. The car was already out of control and sliding tail-first down a steep incline. She hadn't had time to be frightened when the rear end slammed into something with enough force to throw her against the steering wheel.

Whitney sat for long moments while the vehicle came to a shuddering halt. After the creaks and groans died away, she lifted her head in a dazed motion and gulped in a breath of air. What had happened? she wondered.

Her hands were shaking uncontrollably as she struggled with the door latch. Finally she managed to open it and pull herself out of the tilted car.

Rain was still pouring, drenching her white cotton blouse and tan slacks. Whitney was hardly aware of the discomfort. She was in a total state of shock as she looked at her beautiful white Jaguar.

It had slammed into the trunk of a huge pine tree, and was now sitting at a cockeyed angle. The back was smashed into tiny little wrinkles that radiated out across the trunk into bigger, uglier wrinkles.

She wanted to weep at the sight. Instead she cursed and looked up the incline. The car's condition had to be the least of her worries now.

Whitney was cold, hungry and tired. She was also stranded on a lonely, deserted road with no earthly idea of where she was, or what she was going to do.

Rain continued to wash over her, plastering her black hair to her head. Hurriedly, she climbed back into the car, slammed the door shut, then fell back against the seat with a frustrated thump.

She was out of breath and shivering, and she hugged her arms around herself as she tried to think. One thing was certain, she couldn't drive out of here. Even if the car could still run, it wouldn't pull up such a steep, muddy hill.

No, she was going to have to walk, she thought grimly. But not in this rainstorm. She'd sit it out in the car until the storm broke, and then she'd walk to find help.

What seemed like hours later, Whitney was curled up on the front seat, dozing fitfully as the rain still drummed on the roof of the car.

A thumping noise invaded her tired brain. Groaning, she turned her head first one way and then the other. She was too sleepy to wake up and investigate the sound. It was probably just more of those pinecones, she thought, plopping against the hood, adding more damage to her beloved car.

"Hey in there! Are you all right?"

The voice caused Whitney to bolt upright. Someone was out there! A human being had actually found her!

Quickly she rolled down the window. A man's head was bent down, peering at her. The first two things that Whitney noted was a gray cowboy hat and the flashlight he was aiming just below her wide brown eyes.

"I—I had an accident," she blurted out.

"Yes, I can see that, ma'am," he said in a slow Louisiana drawl. "Are you okay?"

Whitney had now gathered her senses together somewhat. She looked back at the man, trying to see his face. It was still inky black outside and he had the advantage of the flashlight. "Yes, I'm all right," she answered. "But I'm stranded. Can you pull me out of here?"

He backed away and swept the light back and forth along the Jaguar. Stepping back up to the window, he said, "Not if you want to ruin what's left of your car."

Whitney groaned and struggled to keep from cursing in front of the stranger. "I've got to get out of here. I'm tired and miserable. Could you possibly call a tow truck for me? I'd be glad to pay you for your troubles."

"Ma'am, I wouldn't want your money. Anyway, you're at least twenty miles from a tow truck. And they wouldn't want to come out on a night like this."

Wouldn't want to come out? Didn't people around here work when duty called? she wondered in outrage. "You must be kidding, aren't you? I'd double his fee."

Whitney could hear a faint laugh in the man's voice as he said, "I doubt old Spider would care if you offered him five hundred dollars. He takes his sleep time real serious, you see. Besides, it would be better to wait until daylight to pull the car out. Otherwise, it might get torn up more than it already is."

Whitney took a deep breath. "Well, I'm sure there must be more than one wrecker service around here, other than this Spider person," she said with her most haughty Eastern accent.

Whitney was certain the amusement deepened in the man's voice as he replied, "Yes, ma'am, there are several wrecker services in Natchitoches. But we aren't in Natchitoches. So I'd suggest you getting out of there and coming home with me."

The air rushed from Whitney's lungs like a popped balloon.

"I—I beg your pardon?" she stammered.

"Look, Miss...?"

"Drake," she quickly supplied. "Whitney Drake."

"Look, Miss Whitney, you're in Louisiana now, not New York. People around here are asleep at this time of night. Especially when it's dark and raining."

She looked at his face. The most she could see was the brim of his hat, which was dripping with rain, a thick, sandy-colored mustache, and a yellow rain slicker. "And I suppose if I'd been lying out here broken and bleeding you'd be reluctant to wake anyone up?" she asked sarcastically.

"Well, now, Miss Whitney, that's just not the case at all, is it? 'Cause you don't look like you have anything broken or bleeding."

Whitney wanted to scream with frustration. "Look, Mr., er..."

"Jones," he put in. "Caleb Jones."

"Mr. Jones," she repeated pointedly, "I don't know you. I can't just leave my car and go with you. For all I know you could be dangerous."

To Whitney's surprise, his low chuckle rumbled through the window. "I can assure you, Miss Whitney, that I'm as harmless as a little ol' flea on a hound's back."

She had to stifle a moan. Harmless, maybe. But certainly as irritating as a flea, she thought.

The man thrust the flashlight through the window, stepped back and opened his slicker wide for her inspection.

"Here, look me over," he told her. "See if I look safe enough."

She took the light and swept it up and down the length of him. He was a tall devil, she noticed. Light-colored hair curled beneath the brim of his hat. His mustache was in definite need of a trim.

As Whitney pointed the light downward she could see he was wearing some type of khaki shirt. A shiny oval badge was pinned to the pocket over his left breast.

"You—you're an officer of the law?" she asked in an astounded voice.

He grinned at her, and Whitney suddenly realized this man was young. Probably not much older than her twenty-eight years. At the moment his eyes were squinted. The only thing she could tell about them was that they were of a light color and edged with thick brown lashes. He had strong white teeth, a full lower lip and a dented chin that had a stubborn look about it.

"Game warden, Miss Whitney."

"Oh," she said, unimpressed. "You're one of those people who look after the birds, the animals and the fish?"

One corner of his mustache lifted mockingly. "Something like that. Something like that and a lot more. But you'd hardly be interested in that, now would you," he said, his voice filled with amusement. He reached down and opened the car door. "Are your bags in the back?"

She nodded and handed the flashlight back to him. "All except this small one in the back seat."

"You'd better get it, cause it sure looks like you won't be getting into the trunk. Not tonight at least."

It was obvious that Mr. Caleb Jones expected her to just go with him. As Whitney mulled the situation over in her mind, she decided there wasn't much of an alternative. If she didn't go with him it would mean spending the rest of the night on the car seat, which was not a very appealing prospect.

"What about your wife and family, Mr. Jones? I don't want to take up needed space."

"That's not a problem," he told her. "I'm not married. I live alone."

Whitney swallowed nervously. She wasn't certain she liked this idea. But what else could she do? she argued with herself. Besides, the man was a law officer. Surely she could trust him.

With that last thought in mind, she quickly handed him the small overnight case before she had the chance to change her mind. After gathering up her purse from the floorboard, she climbed out and stood on the ground beside him.

It was still raining, and her clothes quickly became soaked again as the two of them climbed the steep incline to the road. When they reached the top, Caleb Jones opened the door on a four-wheel drive pickup. It was dark-colored and mud-splattered. Whitney could barely make out some sort of government emblem on the side of the door.

Whitney climbed inside and he set her case at her feet, then shut the door. While he went around to his side and climbed behind the wheel, Whitney glanced around her.

A gunrack was attached to the back window. It was filled with high-powered, deadly looking rifles. Beside her on the seat was some sort of pistol sheathed in a leather holster. Guns terrified Whitney and she wondered why someone who looked after wildlife would need such an arsenal.

She looked over at Caleb as he was reaching for a hand mike that was attached to a two-way radio on the dashboard.

"Mabel," he said without adding any professional jargon, "I'm back. It was a woman."

The radio crackled with static and then a woman's voice sounded. "Do you need an ambulance out there, Caleb?"

Caleb looked over at his passenger. There was a glint in his eyes that made Whitney stiffen her shoulders and toss back her drenched black hair.

"No. She's fine. Just a bit wet. I'm going to take her home with me."

There was a muffled snicker, then, "I'm sure you'll take good care of her, Caleb."

After he returned the mike to its resting place, Whitney asked in a cool voice. "What is that woman insinuating?"

Caleb looked over at her, his brows arched with feigned ignorance. "Insinuating? What do you mean?"

Whitney pursed her lips together. "The tone of her voice. Are you...supposed to be some kind of local Casanova?"

Caleb threw back his head and laughed, making Whitney's face turn red. She was certainly glad it was dark. She hadn't blushed in years, and it embarrassed her to know she was doing it now.

"Miss Whitney, what do they feed you up there in the north? You take things too seriously."

She'd been accused of that before. More than once. But it irked her to hear this man say it. He didn't even know her for goodness sake! Was she that transparent?

"I didn't imagine the intonation of that woman's voice."

Caleb grinned. "Mabel is a real romantic," he explained. "She also has a soft spot for me. Trouble is, she's thirty years older, and I've always had a hankering for kids. So since Mabel's past the age of birthing I decided I just couldn't give her my heart."

Whitney curbed the urge to roll her eyes. "I'm sure that was traumatic for her," she said dryly.

"Hmm. I just hate breaking women's hearts. Just really hate it," he conceded.

Whether he was serious or joking, Whitney could have told him she wasn't in the mood for any of his backwoods philosophy. But Caleb went on before she had a chance to make any kind of comment. "What happened with the car?"

Whitney gripped the armrest as the truck drove over a rough spot in the road. "Basically I was trying to turn around."

"Decided you were on the wrong road, I suppose."

Whitney frowned with disgust. "For the third time to-day. I'd planned on being in Natchitoches tonight."

"Natchitoches is east of here. About twenty miles to the edge, more if you want to go downtown."

"East!" Whitney looked at him as if he'd lost his mind. "I came from the east! How could I have missed it?"

He shrugged as he down-shifted the truck. "Beats the hell out of me, Miss Whitney."

Whitney looked over at him once again. He'd just naturally assumed he could call her Whitney. Still, he added the respectful "Miss" in front of it; she assumed that was common manners down here. Even so, it irked Whitney that this man behaved as if being familiar with her was his prerogative. Not that Whitney was a snob. It was more that she wanted to be in control of things. Always.

The next minute they made a sharp turn to the right and Whitney became aware that they'd entered a cleared area in the woods. As the headlights of the truck swept in front of them, she caught a glimpse of two houses. From what little she could see in the dark, they appeared to be old farmhouses. Plank porches, tin roofs and wooden screen doors reminded her she was in the South. Something like a hundred and fifty yards separated the two houses. Whitney wondered which one belonged to Caleb Jones.

She quickly found out as he pulled to a stop in front of the one to Whitney's right.

"Here we are," he announced as he shut off the motor. "Nothing fancy, but you should be more comfortable here than in your car."

"Who lives over there?" she asked, nodding her head toward the other house.

"That's my neighbor, Pearl."

He said the word neighbor unlike any way Whitney had heard it said before, as if the person was a relative or a very dear friend. Whitney didn't know her neighbors, and as far as she was concerned, she liked it that way.

Not waiting for him to come around and help her, she opened the door and slid out. She'd just reached for her case when he walked up behind her.

"Here," he said, reaching for the small leather suitcase in her hand. "Let me take that for you."

"Thank you," she said, releasing the handle.

"Watch your step," he said, taking hold of her arm with his free hand as they started toward the house. "I don't have a yard light. Pearl and I talked it over and decided we didn't want one."

Whitney mulled over his words as they walked across the small yard and onto the wooden porch. Obviously he and Pearl were close. She was probably one of those curvy, Daisey Mae types. What other kind of woman would live in these backwoods? she asked herself.

"It's not locked. Go on in," he told her once they reached the door. "The light switch is on the left."

Whitney pulled open the screen door and reached for the switch, then blinked as the bright overhead light flooded the room.

"I'm not much of a housekeeper, Miss Whitney," he said, striding across the room. "You'll have to pardon the mess."

Whitney suddenly felt a pang of remorse. This man was opening his home to her and being gracious about it. She couldn't imagine anyone back home doing such a thing. Besides, it wasn't Caleb Jones's fault that she'd crunched her Jaguar into a pine tree.

"Please don't apologize," she said, glancing around the room. It wasn't what you'd call dirty. The linoleum floor was clean, so was the simple furniture. Yet the clothes, newspapers and dirty dishes strewn here and there gave it

an untidy appearance. "You weren't exactly expecting
company," she said, bringing her eyes back to him.

He took off his hat and hung it on a hall tree. It was then
that Whitney noticed that the holstered pistol she'd seen on
the pickup seat was now slung across his shoulder. She
watched him place it carefully on a small oak desk, then
shrug out of his slicker.

Whitney had guessed right about his being tall. He had
to be at least an inch or two over six feet. He was also lean
and fit. Broad shoulders filled out the uniform-type shirt
and blue jeans covered his long, muscular legs.

He was one of those rugged, outdoor men who had
never entered into Whitney's day-to-day living. She really
didn't know what to make of this one, except that he had
a drawl to his voice that raised the hair on the back of her
neck, and that he expected her to trust him like an old,
dear friend.

God knew she wouldn't have trusted a Manhattan policeman enough to go home with him! Why was she trust-
ing this one? she desperately asked herself.

Caleb also hung the slicker on the hall tree, then looked
over at her with an easy grin. "I'm always ready for the
unexpected. It goes with the job."

He grabbed her case again and started toward the other
end of the room. Motioning for Whitney to follow, he
said, "Come along and I'll show you where the extra bedroom is, and where you can wash up."

There was only one bathroom. It was tiny and jammed
between two bedrooms, one of which he pointed out would
be hers. It consisted of more linoleum on the floor, a double bed with an iron bedstead and a small chest of drawers
made of some sort of dark wood. A rag rug lay on the
floor beside the bed; its multi colors clashed with the
patchwork quilt on the bed.

"I'm sure this isn't what you're used to, Miss Whitney, but you're welcome to it."

He set her case on the foot of the bed. Whitney stood to one side of the room, watching him between lowered lashes. Now that they were in the house and out of the dark, she noticed that he moved with a casual, nonchalant grace. His hair was curly enough to be considered unruly and was exactly the same sandy color as his mustache. At the moment his hair was lying in wet, curling tendrils against his collar.

Whitney moistened her lips, then smiled tentatively. "I'm sure it will be fine, Mr. Jones."

He chuckled. "Mr. Jones." He rolled the name over his tongue as if he were savoring the flavor of a fine wine. "Sounds nice. But not many women call me Mr. Jones. Why don't you just make it Caleb?"

Whitney wondered what most women did call him, if it wasn't Mr. Jones, then scolded herself for the question. It hardly mattered to her. All she cared about was a few hours sleep, getting her car back on the highway, and being on her way.

"All right," she replied. "Thank you, Caleb, for coming to my rescue."

The smile on his face broadened, dimpling his right cheek. "My pleasure, Miss Whitney. Now if you'll excuse me, I'll let you freshen up while I find us something to eat."

Before Whitney could tell him she didn't want to eat, he was out the door. Sighing wearily, she made her way to the bathroom.

In the mirror covering the medicine chest, a stranger stared back at Whitney. Her face was white with exhaustion. What little makeup she'd been wearing had been washed away long ago by the rain. Her black hair, which was bobbed, now hung in soggy, limp strands about her head.

She took a comb from her purse and quickly did her best to untangle her hair. Once she had it slicked neatly back from her face, she washed her hands and face, then dried them on a towel hanging near the bathtub.

It smelled like a man. Tangy and spicy. The scent matched Caleb Jones, she decided. He was certainly all man—but definitely not Whitney's type. Not that any type was her type, she thought. She'd had one taste of romance in her life, and God forbid, that one time had been enough for Whitney Drake.

Chapter Two

She found Caleb Jones in the kitchen. It was a small room, consisting of a wooden table and chairs, a gas range, a refrigerator and one wall of pine cabinets. The curtains over the windows were faded red gingham. Otherwise, the room was colorless. So much for his decorating taste, she thought dryly.

"There's no need to fix anything for me," she told him. "I'm not all that hungry."

He turned to look at her as he brought down a box of crackers from the cabinet. "Sure you are," he drawled. "You shouldn't go to bed on an empty stomach."

Whitney wondered how he knew her stomach was empty, but refrained from asking. He'd probably tell her he'd heard it growling.

"Where are you from, Miss Whitney? New York City? Albany? Buffalo?" he asked as he walked over to the table and placed the crackers in the middle.

Before she could answer he was already on his way back to the cabinets. She watched him walk, wondering how he could be so light on his feet in a pair of high-heeled cowboy boots.

"Manhattan," she replied.

"Is that right," he commented. "I was there once. Some of us Louisiana lawmen went up there to see how the big city cops do things."

"I suppose you came away thinking your way was the best way?" she asked.

He turned his head and grinned at her. "Now, Miss Whitney, do I look that narrow-minded?"

Actually he didn't look narrow-minded at all. In spite of his slow voice and easy movements, Whitney had a feeling he didn't miss anything that was going on around him.

"No. You just look like a man who has his own ideas about things."

The grin remained on his mouth. "I like to describe myself as strong-minded."

Whitney just bet he did. The easy arrogance she'd heard in his voice earlier out there on the muddy road had told her that much.

"Do you like sardines, Miss Whitney?" He was taking down a flat tin can from the cabinet along with a jar of mustard.

She answered, "I've never eaten sardines. Are they anything like caviar?"

He chuckled under his breath. "I've never eaten caviar. But I somehow doubt the two could be similar. At least costwise."

"Would you...is there something I can do?" she asked, unsure of what he expected of her. She was at a total loss in the kitchen. There'd always been servants around to do all those things for her, but Caleb Jones hardly knew that. Or did he?

Caleb glanced at her as he placed the mustard and the tin of sardines on the table. He figured she was somewhere past twenty-five, but at the moment she reminded him of a lost little girl. A little bit scared. A little bit defiant. And a whole lot vulnerable.

"Go ahead and have a seat," he told her gently. "You look pretty dead on your feet. Have you been traveling far?"

Whitney gratefully pulled out a chair and seated herself at the table. "Since early this morning," she answered. "I was traveling in Mississippi yesterday."

He was rummaging around in the refrigerator now. Whitney watched him drag out two bottles of beer, a chunk of cheese and a tomato.

"Well, spring is a nice time for vacationing—not too hot, and here in the South the azaleas are beautiful at this time of the year. But there's always the rain to put up with, too."

Whitney hadn't really been thinking about the flowers or the rain when she'd left New York City. But this man would hardly understand. He seemed like the type who was incessantly happy. Things had probably never gone wrong for him. He appeared too self-assured to let them, she thought.

He tossed a couple of paper plates down on the table, two forks and two paper towels, then shoved half toward Whitney. Back at the counter, he quartered the tomato and hacked off a few hunks of cheese. When everything was on the table, he sat down across from her with a smug smile. The way he looked, Whitney thought, one would have thought he'd just prepared a gourmet meal.

"There's nothing like coming home and eating after a hard day's work," he said while busily filling his plate.

"Do you work hard?" she asked, not really knowing what else to say.

His smile was rather wicked looking, she decided. His eyes were grayish blue but there was an ever present gleam in them that made the subdued color glow with inner warmth.

"My counterparts might argue that matter," he told her. "Some days I don't do a blessed thing but drive around the parishes and let my presence be known."

"Sounds very demanding," she said dryly.

"Well," he explained, a complacent smile on his face, "authority speaks for itself. I don't have to do much to keep everyone in line around here."

Whitney tentatively tasted one of the sardines, grimaced, then reached for the mustard. "I thought you only kept the wildlife in line."

He chomped down on a cracker, then washed it down with the cold beer before he answered. "Now that, Miss Whitney, is a big misconception with a lot of people. You see, this badge on my chest means I have the same authority as any other state law officer. In some cases, even more. State game rangers deal in all sorts of crimes, including gun and narcotic trafficking. It just depends on what's going on in the area."

She looked at him with new eyes. So this man put himself in danger. Somehow that didn't surprise her. Whitney had a feeling Caleb Jones was scared of nothing or no one.

"You...weren't wearing your gun. Earlier, I mean," she said.

The dimple appeared in his cheek again, as if her observation amused him. "I wasn't really expecting to run into marauders this close to home. I cheated and took it off."

He gave her a little wink, then went on, "I've been running the lakes the last couple of days. Fishermen aren't really dangerous people, and I don't see any need to lug a gun around on my hip while I hand out poaching tickets, but to stay true to the rules I wear it anyway."

"Poaching? I didn't know there was anything illegal about fishing?"

Caleb slathered a sardine with mustard while thinking he suspected this woman didn't know the first thing about fishing or the outdoors, period. Her skin was milk white and looked as soft as satin. If she worked at anything, it was at something in an office. But from the looks of her clothes, her jewelry and her car, he doubted she had to work at all.

"Everything has rules," he said. "Even fishing. There's a certain limit to how many a person is allowed to catch and keep in his possession. Then some types of fish can only be kept if they measure a certain length. For example, in some lakes a black bass must be ten inches in length, in others twelve or fourteen."

Whitney reached for the beer bottle, deciding she would at least try it. She didn't drink beer, but he obviously expected her to. And she didn't want to appear ungracious by ignoring it.

The cap was a twist-off type. Whitney struggled with it for a moment before Caleb leaned across the table and took it from her.

"Let me do that for you," he told her. "You're going to hurt yourself with that thing."

One little twist from his strong fingers had the cap off. Whitney thanked him as he handed the cold bottle back to her.

The brew had a tart, strong taste but Whitney discovered it went well with the crackers and sardines. After a moment she said, "Back to the fish. What do you do, go around measuring them?" The question sounded inane, she thought, but then so did his laws.

"That's exactly what I do if I think a catch is illegal." He leaned his chair back on its hind legs and folded his hands across his midsection as he looked at her.

Whitney found his gaze disarming and she hoped he wasn't aware of it. She'd met all types of men in her life, but none of them had been capable of ruffling her. She couldn't understand why this one did. Unless it was the circumstances that had thrown them together. The easy, familiar way he had with her wasn't helping things, either, she thought a little desperately.

"What do you do if you find someone with an illegal catch?" she asked, chewing slowly and precisely.

"Fine them. Seventy-five dollars a fish."

Flabbergasted, Whitney stared at him. "That much? Just for one little fish?"

He let his chair back down with a soft thump. "That's right," he answered, then openly grinned at her. "And I'm sure that right about now you're thinking that's a lot of money for something as trivial as a fish."

Whitney cleared her throat, embarrassed that he could read her so easily. "Well, it does seem rather ridiculous."

The humor left Caleb's face as he reached for his beer. "Our lakes, fish and waterfowl are an important part of our country's resources. And anyone in my parishes better respect that idea, or they'll pay with money—or their time in jail."

"You sound very dedicated to your job," she said.

There was a subtle lift to his brows as his eyes leveled on her once again. "I am. That's why I do what I do," he replied. "What do you do, Miss Whitney?"

Her fingers suddenly gripped the neck of the beer bottle. She looked down and away, anywhere but at him. "Presently nothing. I'm...I'm on vacation, remember?"

Caleb's eyes narrowed as he watched her fingers nervously twine together. "I remember *me* saying you were on vacation, not you," he reminded her.

He was too damn smart, she thought, jerking her face back up to meet his glance. "I *am* on vacation," she said a bit too defensively. "It just happens to be a forced one. I was fired from my job."

"You worked?"

"Of course, I worked!" she snapped. "What did you think I did?"

He held up a pleading palm. "Now, Miss Whitney, don't let your Yankee hackles stand on end."

She let out a long breath. He was probing into a raw wound, prying it apart just enough to let out all the anger she'd been bottling inside her for the past week. Thing was, he didn't even know it, she thought. "I'm not stupid," she said offhandedly, some of her temper waning.

"Who said you were?"

Oh, no, she thought grittily. She wasn't about to let this man maneuver her into talking about herself, her job—or her lack of a job. "Look, I'm very good at what I do," she blurted out, feeling the insane need to defend herself to this man.

"No doubt," he drawled. "Is that why you were fired?"

Her blood felt as if it were boiling. She thrust her fingers through her damp hair, then pinned a cutting look on him. "I was fired because my father owns the company," she said, unable to keep the nastiness from her voice.

"Relatives can be hell at times," he said.

His comment was so far from what she'd been expecting that she suddenly wanted to both laugh and cry. Resisting the urge to do either, she rose from the table, her arms hugging her slender waist. She stood there looking down at him. "Living can be hell, Mr. Jones."

He shook his head and clucked his tongue. "The name is Caleb," he reminded her. "And you've come to the right place."

She grimaced, and stepping away from the table turned her back to him. "For what?" she muttered wearily.

Whitney was unaware that he'd risen to his feet until his hand touched her arm. She jerked around violently, causing his lips to twist into a wry smile.

"To learn what living is all about," he answered easily.

She laughed harshly. "Have you forgotten? I'm here because my Jaguar is sitting out there somewhere smashed into a pine tree, it's raining, and Spider doesn't care whether he works or not. That's why I'm here!"

His big hand lifted and touched her cheek. Whitney wanted to leap back away from him, but forced herself to stay put.

"Miss Whitney," he said softly, "you need to go to bed, let those sardines and beer settle, let yourself listen to the rain on the roof. Everything is going to be all right."

Whitney was suddenly frightened, not of Caleb Jones but of herself. She was having the crazy urge to lean into this man, to lay her head against his shoulder and weep.

She couldn't let that happen. She had to be strong or he would see how heartbroken and frightened she really was.

"How can you say that? You don't know anything about it." He was so close that she could see the pores in his skin, the flecks of slate gray in his eyes. The unique and mysterious scent of his hair and skin drifted to her nostrils, teasing her senses. She breathed in deeply and the corner of his mustache lifted cockily.

"I don't have to know. Down here in the South we dance to a different tune, Miss Whitney. You'll like it. It's slow and easy." His forefinger slid up and down her cheek. "Soft and warm, like a lazy river on a summer's day."

Whitney's heart banged in her chest like that of a trapped bird. She backed away from him, her eyes wide open. "I—I'm tired," she said, her voice barely above a whisper. "If you don't mind, I'm going to bed."

Before he had time to reply, she turned and fled to the bedroom, shutting the door behind her. For long moments she leaned against it, breathing deeply, willing her shaken senses to pull themselves back together.

Tomorrow, she promised herself. Tomorrow, she'd have her car back. Crunched up or not, she would drive it as it was. She wanted to be out of here and back on the road.

Her trembling legs carried her to the bed. She sat down on the edge and quickly rummaged in her purse for a cigarette.

Not until she'd lit it and inhaled deeply did she let herself recall the moment Caleb Jones had touched her. Her senses were still splintered in all sorts of directions. The feeling confused and frightened her, especially now that it was dawning on her just how much she'd wanted to touch him back.

Careful, Whitney, she told herself. If you don't watch yourself you'll be running from more than your lost ambitions. You'll wind up running from a man with a cocky grin and gleaming blue eyes.

There was nothing like sleep, Whitney thought, snuggling her head deeper into the pillow. Peaceful, uninterrupted sleep. A comfortable bed. No city traffic or alarms buzzing to jolt her awake.

No city traffic, her fuzzy mind repeated. The next second she bolted upright and stared dazedly around the room.

Bright sunlight was streaming through the open window. Beyond the screen she could hear birds chirping and singing and farther beyond, a rooster crowing.

Groaning, she pushed back the sheet and quilt and swung her feet to the cool floor. She remembered everything now. The wreck, the rain and the man.

Now it appeared she'd overslept. Quickly she groped around in her handbag until she pulled out a small wristwatch. Nine-thirty, she read. Was it that late? She'd never slept that late before. How could life go blithely on while she'd been asleep?

Rushing now, she tossed off her silk nightshirt and pulled on the rumpled clothes she'd worn yesterday. Since her bags were still in her wrecked car, she hardly had any choice in the matter of her wardrobe. After thoroughly brushing her hair, she opened the bedroom door and stepped out.

"Caleb?" she called, glancing out toward the living room. "Are you there?"

Instinctively she knew he was gone. The house was too quiet and empty-feeling. Sighing, she went back inside the bedroom and collected her toiletries from her overnight case.

A few minutes later she came out of the bathroom feeling more refreshed. She'd applied a small amount of makeup and gathered her thick hair at the back of her neck with a dark blue scarf. At least she looked more rested and presentable even if her clothes looked as if they'd been through a paper press.

Whitney discovered the note in the kitchen. It was propped against the salt shaker, on the table where they'd eaten.

Miss Whitney,
Spider is on his way to pull out your car. I thought I'd go on down there and see to things for you. Make yourself at home. You're welcome to anything you can find in the kitchen. Or if you want, just wander over to Pearl's. She'll be happy to feed you.

It was signed simply, "Caleb." Whitney stared at the note, wondering why he hadn't woken her. After all, it was her car, her problem. And when was he coming back?

"'Wander over to Pearl's,'" she repeated aloud. Good Lord, the man was strange, she thought. Did he expect her to walk over to a stranger's house and ask for breakfast? She'd heard of Southern hospitality before, but surely they didn't stretch things that far down here in the woods.

Whitney walked around the kitchen, catching signs of Caleb's earlier presence—a plate dirtied with egg yolk and toast crumbs, a jar of strawberry jam left open on the table, a crumpled napkin.

The man was obviously a breakfast eater, she concluded, and he could cook something besides sardines and crackers. She looked around the small room, feeling his presence even though he wasn't there. It made her uncomfortable and she forced the image of his easy smile and the memory of his slow voice to the back of her mind.

Opening the cabinets, she began to search for something to eat, something that required little preparation. Whitney was lucky. She found a box of cornflakes on the top shelf. Now if the man had sugar and milk she'd be in business.

The sugar bowl was on the gas range. Whitney placed it, along with a bowl of the flakes and a spoon, on the table. Back at the refrigerator she looked for a carton or plastic jug of milk and found neither. What she did find was a gallon jar filled with some sort of white liquid.

Whitney stared at it warily, then decided to take it out and examine it. Perhaps it was milk, she thought hopefully. Maybe his carton had leaked and he poured the contents into the glass container.

She opened the lid and sniffed, then instantly realized the two-inch yellow stuff on top must be cream. Was this stuff soured? Whitney didn't know why it would be separated, but when she sniffed it again, she knew it wasn't spoiled.

Deciding she was too hungry to ask questions, she found a spoon and stirred it all together. Before she could change her mind she poured it over the cornflakes and dipped in her spoon. It was milk, she decided as she chewed, just not the kind she was accustomed to.

She was halfway through the bowl of flakes when she realized her morning coffee was missing. That was one thing she did know how to make.

Whitney went over to the cabinet to find the makings, then discovered she didn't have to. At the end of the cabinet counter, a stainless-steel percolator was plugged into the wall. It was full of fresh, hot coffee.

Just as she was reaching for an empty cup, a loud bark sounded right beside her. The unexpected noise caused her to jerk and yell with fright. She whirled around to see a dog standing at the back door, his black nose pressed against the screen. She let out a long sigh.

"Where did you come from?" she asked the dog.

The question brought a series of deep yelps, accompanied by several scratches on the door. Whitney eyed the animal with misgivings. She knew very little about dogs, and absolutely nothing about this monstrous, blood-hound-looking thing.

"I guess you know I'm a stranger, don't you?" she questioned the dog again.

He barked louder this time and clawed at the door with both front paws. Whitney decided the best thing to do was get her coffee and leave the room so he couldn't see her. Otherwise, he was going to tear the whole door down. Long, sharp dog fangs sinking into her leg or throat wasn't exactly what she needed to go along with all the other problems she had at the moment.

By the time Whitney had started on her second cup of coffee it was ten-thirty. She was growing more frustrated and nervous with each passing minute. Where was the man? How long did it take to tow one small car from a ditch? She wanted to be gone from here. The sooner the better.

She smoked five cigarettes, then angry with herself, tossed down the near-empty pack and went back to the bedroom.

Whitney wasn't exactly trained in the art of bedmaking, but she forced herself to make it look as smooth as it had been when she'd climbed into it. After she'd finished that task, she packed what few little belongings she had back into the overnight case and carried it out to the living room. She wanted to be ready to leave when Caleb returned.

Chapter Three

It was an hour later before Caleb's truck finally pulled to a stop in front of the house. Whitney let out a sigh of relief as she watched him climb out of the truck and walk to the house.

"Where have you been?" she blurted out as soon as he hit the porch.

He stopped dead in his tracks, looked at her through the screen door, then smiled beguilingly. "Good morning to you, too, Miss Whitney. Did you have a good sleep? I didn't know you were going to miss me so, or I would've woken you up and taken you with me."

She wanted to scream at him. Instead she took another deep breath. "I thought you realized I was in a hurry to get my car?"

He pushed open the door and stepped past her into the house. She turned to look at him, realizing that he had on fresh clothes that looked starched and ironed. His jaws had that shiny, just-shaven look, and a spicy scent followed in his wake. He made her feel very rumpled and unkempt.

"What for?" he asked easily.

What for? Was the man crazy? Her eyes opened wide. "Have you forgotten that I'm stranded here?"

"So. If you weren't here, where would you be?"

She opened her mouth, closed it, then opened it again. "That is beside the point," she snapped. "I have things to do, places to go. And most of all I need my things from the trunk."

He smiled again, this time smugly. "They're in the back of my truck. All four cases. I'll bring them in for you in a minute."

"Bring them in!" she repeated. "What are you talking about? I want my car. I want to get out of here."

"Why? Don't you like it here?"

The urge to groan and shout overwhelmed her. All she could do was look at him and shake her head. "That is beside the point, too," she finally managed to say, reaching for her handbag and the nearly empty pack of cigarettes.

Caleb watched her light the tobacco with shaking hands. He'd never seen anyone so nervous. She was like a rocket, ready to take off in flight at any given moment. It was difficult for Caleb to relate to such high-strung emotion. Not that he didn't live under pressure at times. He just happened to react to it differently.

She exhaled a lungful of smoke, then went on, waving the hand with the cigarette through the air with short, choppy movements. "Don't you understand that I'm traveling? When a person is traveling his objective is to get down the road."

Caleb hooked his hands over the gunbelt at his hips as he watched her through narrowed, speculative eyes. "Not necessarily," he said. "Some people like to make stops and smell the flowers along the way."

Yes, he would, she thought dryly. This was the second time he'd mentioned flowers in the very few short hours she'd known him. But it was probably only the second time in the past year that Whitney had thought of them.

"That might be true," she conceded. "But I'm not into flowers."

Frowning, he started toward the kitchen. "Well, you should be," he tossed back at her.

Whitney followed him, puffing heavily on the cigarette. "I'm not a romantic like that Mabel person you were talking to last night. Flowers are the least of my worries," she said. "Besides," she added with a shrug, "I don't have time for smelling flowers. They don't last, so what's the use."

Grimacing, he shook his head and looked around the kitchen. "Did you have breakfast?"

"Cornflakes and whatever that white stuff in the glass jar was."

He cocked an eyebrow at her. "Around here that stuff is called milk. Fresh, whole milk, right from the cow. One of my friends has a milk cow. He's kind enough to keep me supplied."

Whitney darted him a stunned look. "Right from the cow? You mean it hasn't been homogenized, or whatever it is they do to kill the germs?"

Caleb snorted. "What germs? Do I look like I've been infected with germs?"

In spite of willing them not to, Whitney felt her eyes glide over him. He looked like a vital, healthy, red-blooded male. She took another long drag from the cigarette. "Never mind. It's probably no worse than breathing Manhattan smog."

He gave her a pointed look. "I really doubt it, Miss Whitney," he drawled.

She walked over to the double sink, smashed her cigarette in it, then tossed the butt into a garbage pail. Caleb watched her movements, thinking how thin and fragile she looked. There was an unhealthy paleness to her skin and he wondered if she'd recently been ill.

"Where is my car now?" she asked, turning back to him, a determined look on her face. "Wherever it is, I want you to take me there."

Patiently he walked over to her and took her by the arm. The muscles under his fingers were taut and stiff as he led her over to the table and chairs.

"Sit down, Miss Whitney. I swear to God, you're wearing me out just watching you."

And he was wearing her down with his slow, calm ways, she thought desperately. Sighing, she sat down on the edge of a chair and looked up at him. "Okay, I'm still. Now about my car."

"Your car is at Spider's body shop."

"And where is that?"

"Oh, about ten miles from here. West a little, then north a little."

His vagueness irritated her even more. "I'm packed and ready to go. Is there a problem?"

He rubbed his jaw, then pulled out the chair next to her and sat down. "With the car, Miss Whitney. I'm afraid you have a major problem with the car."

She crossed her legs and her toe began to nervously slice the air. "It won't bother me to drive it with dents. I'll have it repaired once I get back to New York."

He folded his arms across his chest as he leveled his eyes on her face. It was a pretty face, he decided, or would be if it wasn't quite so thin. It was dominated by huge brown eyes so dark he hadn't been sure they were brown until this morning when he saw them in the sunlight. Her mouth was wide and expressive, telling him more than she realized. At the moment her lips were pursed together tightly. But Caleb suspected they would be trembling if she'd only let her guard down.

"I'm afraid it's more than dents, Miss Whitney. The driveline was jerked out from under it when you slid down that embankment."

"The driveline? Is that necessary?"

He nodded patiently. "It sets behind the transmission. It's what makes the axles turn, which in turn make the wheels roll."

Her slender shoulders suddenly sagged. "Oh, I see. Well, can this Spider fix it?"

Caleb propped his chair on its hind legs. "Sure he can. Spider can fix anything that's mechanical. He can even take out the dents and paint it for you if you like."

Whitney's face brightened. "Then there's no problem. When will he have it ready to drive?"

"Spider said two weeks. Give or take a day or two."

Whitney jerked upright, a desperate look in her eyes. "You are kidding, aren't you?"

Solemnly he shook his head.

Whitney shot to her feet. "Take me there right now! This whole thing is ridiculous! I'm going to have my car taken to a professional, one who—"

Caleb's hand reached up and pulled her back down onto the chair. "Spider is a professional," he assured her. "You couldn't find a better mechanic if you searched all over the United States."

"But two weeks! The man is crazy!"

"You were driving an expensive, foreign car. You don't find parts for those things just anywhere, certainly not around here. They'll have to be ordered. Shipping them here will take a few days, and then the work to the car itself will take some time. You can't expect miracles, Miss Whitney."

She let out a long breath. Yes, she could see that what he was saying was probably the truth. But still, he couldn't expect her to stay around here. Not for two weeks! She'd be insane by then.

Slowly her hand lifted and pushed back the wave of hair that had dipped across her forehead. "I—I'm sorry, Caleb. You must think I'm an unreasonable person. But this . . . this whole thing is just so frustrating. I'd planned on being at Padre Island by the end of this week."

Her eyes closed momentarily and Caleb noticed how thick and black her lashes were against her pale skin. He realized that from the moment he'd found her in the car last night he'd felt an unreasonable protectiveness toward her, God only knew why. She was nothing like the women he was usually attracted to. She was a sarcastic bundle of nerves. And to top it off, she was a Yankee. Not that he was prejudiced, but Yankee women just didn't understand a Southern man like himself.

She wasn't even a romantic, he thought. She'd told him so herself. Caleb had always thought of himself as a gallant gentleman who still believed in moonlight and roses, courtship and family tradition. Maybe that was a dying art where she came from; he didn't know. And he would probably be safer if he didn't bother himself to find out.

Drawing his attention back to her words, he asked, "What's so important about getting to Padre Island?"

Nothing really, she silently answered. Actually she'd picked up the map and jabbed a finger. It had just happened to land on Padre Island. There was nothing there for her really. Just like there was nothing for Whitney anywhere else in the world. The thought terrified her. But she'd never let this man know that.

"Beaches," she quipped. "Warm, sandy beaches."

"Bull," he scoffed. "You won't find anything there but a bunch of oily tourists."

"How would you know?"

"Because I've been there. Now are you ready for me to bring your things in? I really should be getting to work. Mabel's going to think I've disappeared off the face of the earth if I don't answer my radio soon."

"No. You leave my cases right where they are! If I can't get to Padre Island at least I can rent a motel room in Natchitoches."

"For two weeks?" Caleb got to his feet, towering over her with his six feet two inches. "You're crazy, Miss Whitney. You don't want to be holed up in a motel room for two weeks."

She rose to her feet, also—then wished she hadn't when she realized there was only a matter of inches separating them. "It looks as if I really have no choice in the matter. It's either that, or rent a car. And that idea doesn't appeal to me because I don't want to leave my Jaguar in unknown hands while I go off to another state."

He shook his head. "Of course, you have a choice. You can stay here with me."

"Oh, no. I—I couldn't possibly do that. It's out of the question."

"Why?"

Whitney couldn't believe this man. In all of her life she'd never met one exactly like him. "Why? Several reasons. One, I don't know you. Two, I'd be imposing. Three, you're a man and I'm—"

"A woman," he finished with a grin. "Well, Miss Whitney, that's hardly a big surprise to me."

"Mr. Jones, I—"

"Caleb," he gently reminded her. "After my grandaddy William Caleb Jones. He'd want you to call me Caleb, too."

With utter despair, she covered her eyes with her hands. "Caleb, I can't stay here. So why don't you take me into Natchitoches where I'll be out of your hair and you can forget about the disruption I've caused you."

"It's no disruption. I'm gone the biggest part of the day. You can have the house all to yourself. And I know once you get to know each other, you and Pearl will get along like a house on fire."

Her hands fell away from her face as she looked up at him. There was no reasoning with him. She could see that. He obviously believed he knew what she wanted more than she did herself. What had the Fates done to her? Why had she turned down the road leading to Caleb Jones? she asked herself.

"I'm trying to tell you I can't stay here. I'm a city person. It would—"

Loud barks suddenly interrupted her. Both she and Caleb looked toward the screen door where the dog had reappeared and was now scratching with a vengeance.

"Rebel, get away from there!" Caleb scolded. "Can't you see I'm having a conversation with a lady?"

The dog looked at him and let out a long whine. Determined, Whitney started again. "As I was saying, there wouldn't be anything for me—"

The baying began again. This time Caleb left Whitney and walked over to the dog. Before she knew his intentions, he pushed open the door and Rebel burst through the opening.

Whitney stared wide-eyed as it bounded straight at her.

"Rebel! Rebel, down!"

The dog's front paws landed with a thud on Whitney's chest just before she fainted in a heap on the floor.

"She's so thin, Caleb. It looks like the poor little thing hasn't eaten in days."

"I know, Pearl. I think she's one of those women that starve themselves for fashionable reasons."

The old woman snorted as she stood, hand on hips, staring down at Whitney's inert form on the sofa. Suddenly she glanced over at Caleb who was fumbling with an ammonia capsule he'd found in the first-aid kit from his truck.

"Hurry up with that thing. Land sakes, I might as well slosh some water on her for all the good you're doing," Pearl scolded.

Whitney could hear the voices and even make out the words, but they seemed to be coming from a long distance away. With great effort, she tried to concentrate her energy and open her eyes.

Gently, Caleb lifted Whitney's head beneath his right arm and waved the aromatic spirits under her nose. The result brought first a groan, then a cough and a splutter that had Whitney's eyes flying wide open. "What— Oh, my God," she groaned with embarrassment.

She looked toward the end of the couch. The bloodhound was looking at her, his head cocked, long ears perked, his tongue lolled to one side. Obviously he was a harmless pet.

"Whoa, Miss Whitney. Don't be frightened of Rebel," Caleb told her.

She tried to move upright to a sitting position, but halfway there, she discovered her head was spinning. She fell back helplessly against Caleb's arm. "I'm not frightened now," she added weakly.

This brought a hoot of laughter from Pearl, which made Caleb chuckle under his breath.

Indignant, Whitney looked over at the old woman. She was wearing a gathered skirt made of black cotton printed with tiny red roses, a black shirtwaist blouse buttoned at her elbows and little black granny shoes. She had black hair, also, which was scraped back into a tight little bun at the back of her head. The color looked rather strange considering her age. Whitney was certain the woman couldn't have been a day under seventy-five.

Pearl stepped forward and leaned toward Whitney. "Gal, that dog wouldn't hurt you." She patted Whitney's cheek as if to make sure she was truly awake.

"Rebel likes women," Caleb spoke. "He was just going to say hello. Is that why you fainted? You were afraid of the dog?"

Whitney's head shook back and forth. "I...when I got to my feet I was feeling a little light-headed." She'd thought the dizziness was from frustration at Caleb. But now she wasn't so sure. "And then the dog came at me and . . . everything went black."

"You've been out cold," Caleb informed her. "I think you should see a doctor."

"Doctor, my foot," Pearl barked. "The girl needs rest. She looks worn out. Dark circles under her eyes. Skinny as a gosling. All she needs is good food and a long quiet spell."

That was just what Dr. Bergman back in New York had told her, although he had used different terms. Strange that this old woman she'd never met before came up with the same diagnosis. It had taken several medical tests and a whopping bill before Dr. Bergman had reached those conclusions.

Whitney struggled to a sitting position. Caleb kept a steadying hand on her back. She could feel the warmth of it through her thin shirt and was surprised at how comforting it was to know he was there to catch her if she toppled over again.

"She's right. These past few days I've driven several hundred miles. I—I guess they're catching up with me," Whitney said.

"'Course I'm right," Pearl said, her voice softening in a maternal way. "Now you lean back there, honey, and I'll go fix you something to eat. Caleb, you go get her cases and bring them in. I'll see to Miss Whitney."

Whitney's eyes darted from Pearl's to Caleb's. Why did she feel so utterly helpless around these people? For the past few years *she'd* been the one in charge, the one who'd given orders and seen that things were running smoothly. Had she fallen that flat on the bottom? she wondered with deep despair.

"But I—I was going to Natchitoches," she argued.

Pearl hesitated at the doorway leading into the kitchen. She looked sternly from Whitney to Caleb. "We're not about to let you go to a motel and you not feeling well. In a few days, if you feel like it and still want to, Caleb will take you. Won't you, boy?"

Caleb nodded. "Pearl's right. You can have a quiet rest here while your car's being repaired." The corner of his mustache rose as he smiled and lifted his hand from her back. "And like I told you last night, I'm harmless. Just like ol' Rebel here."

At the sound of his name, the dog came to life. His whole body wiggled and twisted with affection as he sidled up to Whitney's leg.

She looked down at the dog and Caleb said, "He's a real sucker for a female. Go on. Pet him. He likes you."

Whitney was glad someone did. In the past months she'd watched as her many friends dwindled down to one handful. She reached and stroked the dog's head. He nuzzled her hand and wagged his tail, making Whitney feel extremely foolish over her earlier fear.

"He was here this morning when I was eating breakfast," she told Caleb. "I thought he was going to tear down the door."

Caleb chuckled as he moved away from the couch. "He wanted you to let him in. I guess I've spoiled him, but Rebel is my best friend."

Caleb went out and Whitney knew he was going after her suitcases. Resignedly she leaned her head back and closed her eyes. The fainting spell had brought home to her just how tired and rundown her body had become. She'd been fighting the fatigue for some time now. She didn't have the strength to fight it anymore. Certainly not it and Caleb Jones, too. She'd stay here tonight, but after that she'd be on her way, she promised herself.

A few minutes later Caleb drove away in his government truck with the rifles hanging in the back windshield. Whitney stood on the porch and watched him, all the while asking herself why he was being so kind to her. The people she was used to dealing with only gave when they wanted something in return. It made her wonder what Caleb was going to ask from her, and how long it would be before she discovered what it was.

Chapter Four

The truck disappeared from Whitney's view and determinedly she pulled her thoughts away from Caleb Jones. Behind her she could hear the old woman in the kitchen muttering to herself as she pulled pots and pans from the cabinets.

Slowly Whitney walked back inside the house. In the kitchen she found Pearl busily chopping a head of cabbage.

"I'm not really hungry, Pearl," she said. "May I call you Pearl?"

The woman's scrawny hands scraped the cabbage from the chopping board into a blue cooking pot. "I'd like for you to call me Pearl," she said without bothering to look up. "And I'll call you Whitney, if you don't mind. Nothing formal about us around here."

Yes, Whitney could see that. Pearl had come into Caleb's kitchen as though it belonged to her, too. She seemed to know where eveything was. Whitney concluded the woman must be very familiar with Caleb's house and Caleb himself.

"Well, like I said, Pearl, it's only a couple of hours since I had breakfast."

"Cornflakes?" she snorted her disgust. "That ornery Caleb. The least he could have done was fed you before he took off."

Whitney felt her cheeks coloring as she thought about Caleb moving around the house while she lay sleeping. She wondered if he'd looked in on her. God, she certainly hoped not! No man had ever seen her in bed, asleep and with her guard down. It gave her a strange feeling to think that Caleb might have.

"I—I'm afraid I was asleep when Caleb cooked breakfast."

Pearl set the pot of cabbage on the stove and turned on a bright flame beneath it. Back at the cabinet she began to slice meat with a huge butcher knife.

"What is that?" Whitney asked, moving in for a closer inspection.

"Slab bacon. Caleb buys it by the whole slab so he can have thick slices," she told Whitney.

Whitney wondered what all that cholesterol was doing to his system and why someone wasn't warning him about his eating habits.

Pearl placed several slices in a black iron skillet on the stove. Whitney joined her, watching her arrange the meat with a long cooking fork.

"Have you known Caleb long?"

Pearl's little face wrinkled with a broad smile. "I helped with Caleb's birthing. He came out fire engine red and squawling to the top of his lungs. I knew he was gonna be a good one from that very moment."

The meat began to sizzle. Satisfied, Pearl turned down the fire and went to work chopping green onions.

"How long ago was that?" Whitney asked curiously, then wanted to bite her tongue. It wouldn't do to let this old woman think she was interested in him.

"Let's see," she mused aloud. "It'll be thirty-one years come this May. Not all that long ago."

Whitney grinned slightly at Pearl's talking of thirty-one years as though it were just a matter of a few days.

"How old are you, Whitney?"

"Me? I'm twenty-eight."

"You have a man? Kids?"

The faint smile fell from Whitney's lips. Her eyes dropped to the floor as she thought of her broken engagement. It had been eight months since Edward had told her he no longer wanted to marry her. She was over Edward, but she wasn't quite sure she was over being rejected.

Unaware of how her question had affected Whitney, Pearl reached for a pile of dark leaf lettuce.

"No. I've never been married," Whitney replied.

"Well, that's nothing to be ashamed of," Pearl drawled. "I was twenty-five before I married Ben. And believe me, Whitney, back in those days twenty-five and unmarried was scandalous. Mama cried a bucketful of tears over me. By the time I was fifteen she had this farmer over in Texas all picked out for me. But I balked. I wasn't about to marry a man I didn't love. It took me a while to find that special one, but I did."

Whitney could have told her that she wasn't worried about being an old maid, but she didn't have the heart to dispute Pearl's words of wisdom. "Is your husband still living?"

Pearl's head shook. "No. He died ten years ago. Doctor said it was old age. But I'll never believe that. Ben was only eighty."

Rebel appeared in the kitchen. Whitney looked down as the dog whacked his tail affectionately against her leg. Feeling an unaccustomed tenderness toward the animal, she reached down to pet him. She'd heard it said that dogs instinctively knew when a person was good and worthwhile. And she was worthwhile, wasn't she? Her father, her friends, even her fiancé had turned away from her, but maybe the dog could see the things inside her that they couldn't see.

"I suppose you lived here, then?"

Pearl nodded. "Been living here since '35."

Amazed, Whitney stared at the old woman. It was almost impossible for her to believe a person could live in the same exact spot in the woods for fifty-some years.

"That's a long time. Have you ever traveled?"

"Some. We went to California once, Georgia a couple of times. I was always glad to get back home."

Pearl sat the bowl of lettuce and onions to one side. "Well," she said brightly, her quick, birdlike eyes darting over Whitney. "You're looking much better now. A little pink in your cheeks. You really gave Caleb a scare there for a minute."

Whitney felt a rueful smile touch her mouth. "I feel very badly about causing so much trouble. Did Caleb tell you I smashed my car into a tree?"

The woman nodded, then reached over and patted Whitney's arm. "You picked the right place to do it, honey. Caleb will take real good care of you."

Where had she heard that before? Oh, yes, Mabel, the romantic. Whitney wondered if all the women around here doted on Caleb Jones, or just the older ones.

"Actually, Pearl, I've been living on my own for a long time. I'm not used to anyone taking charge over my life. It's not necessary for Caleb to see about my car, or give me a place to stay."

Whitney walked over to the table and took a seat. She was feeling much better now, but her legs still seemed weak and shaky. Rebel plopped down at her feet and a moment later Pearl brought her a cup of fresh coffee.

Whitney accepted it with a grateful smile. "Thank you, Pearl."

"You're welcome, Whitney. And for what it's worth, maybe it's time someone looked after you for a change. Caleb's a man you can lean on. He's got strong, broad shoulders. You don't ever have to worry about him breaking. Guess that's what makes him such a good lawman."

Whitney watched Pearl go back to attending the sizzling bacon. What made the old woman think she needed someone to lean on? Did she look that lost? Whitney wondered. One thing was certain, she had no intention of leaning on Caleb Jones, or any man for that matter.

Pearl's meal consisted of cabbage stewed with bell peppers and onions, a salad drenched with vinegar and wilted with hot bacon drippings. Cornmeal muffins and fried slab bacon rounded out the menu.

Whitney had never seen such food in her life and she wondered desperately how she could get out of eating without hurting Pearl's feelings. But, of course, there wasn't any way to avoid eating after the woman had gone to so much trouble.

Picking up her fork, she tentatively tasted a morsel of the cabbage, then the salad. To her amazement both were rather tasty and she ventured on to the bacon and cornbread. Before she realized it, her plate was empty and she was agreeing to second helpings.

Once the meal was over Pearl shooed her into the living room and ordered her to lie down on the couch. Whitney wanted to argue that she wasn't used to lying down in the middle of the day. She wasn't used to being idle, or the silence of these woods.

For the past few years her life had been nonstop rush—phone calls, business meetings, decisions and contracts to be made. Her body—or her mind—didn't know how to slow down. At least not this slow. But Pearl was adamant, and how did a person argue with someone as old as Pearl? Whitney wondered. It seemed disrespectful somehow.

To please the other woman, Whitney gave in and stretched out on the plaid cushions of the couch, propping her head with a blue throw pillow.

Apparently satisfied that Whitney would stay put, Pearl went about picking up and tidying the house. After a while Whitney closed her eyes and listened as the old woman washed dishes in the kitchen, and sang a hymn under her breath.

Whitney didn't know she'd slept until she woke several hours later to the lengthening shadows of sundown. A light spread had been tucked around her legs.

Her eyes drifted across the room, to where Pearl sat in a bentwood rocker with some sort of hand sewing in her lap. Rebel lay stretched out at her feet and curled up against his midsection was a fat calico cat. It was as if all three were patiently watching over her. The idea gave Whitney a warm, peculiar feeling.

Pushing back the spread, she swung her feet to the floor. "What time is it?" she asked groggily.

Without bothering to look up, Pearl gathered up her sewing and rose from the rocker. She seemed to know that Whitney was awake even before Whitney had known it. "I'd say it was about time for Caleb to be coming home. Should be here any time now."

Sometime during Whitney's sleep the scarf had slipped loose from her hair. She tossed the wayward strands out of her eyes. "I guess I was more tired than I thought."

"Guess you were," Pearl agreed, giving her a critical look over. "You've been sleeping like a baby. Now that you're awake I'm going back to my house. Chester's getting mad and I've got to feed the chickens."

Whitney got to her feet and stretched. She wondered who Chester was, but decided not to ask. It might be a long story and Pearl seemed anxious to leave. "Of course," she told Pearl. "And thank you for the meal."

"It was no trouble," she said, pushing through the screen door. "I'll be seeing you tomorrow."

Whitney had already decided she was going to have Caleb drive her into Natchitoches tomorrow, but she didn't explain this to Pearl. "Yes. Good night," she said, following the old woman out the door.

Dusk was falling over the pines and cypress trees. Whitney watched Pearl walk a beaten track through the mown grass that stretched between the two houses. The calico cat was at her heels. When they reached the house another cat, a black one, pranced across the porch and greeted them. After a moment all three disappeared into the house.

With a restless sigh, Whitney sat down on the top step and looked around her. She'd never been an outdoor person. The few times she'd spent in the woods had been with her father when she'd been a small girl, and he'd owned a cabin in New England.

But Louisiana was nothing like New England. Even though the sky was clear, the humidity was oppressive. It was only the first week in April, and it was already very warm. Yet the weather was not the only difference. There was something isolated and timeless about the dense woods around her.

Whitney was still trying to figure out what made it seem that way when the sound of a motor broke into her thoughts. Eagerly she looked down the dirt road, then quickly told herself it didn't really matter if it was Caleb. He was pesky and arrogant and the less she saw of him the better.

Yet as soon as the truck pulled to a stop something propelled her to her feet. With her hands thrust in the pockets of her slacks, she walked out to meet him.

Caleb grinned out the window at her. "How did your day go, Miss Whitney?"

She couldn't help but smile back at him. Partly because he was still calling her Miss Whitney, and partly because there was something about his boyish grin that got to her in spite of her best efforts to ignore it.

"Don't you think we've known each other long enough for you to call me just Whitney?" she asked him.

He climbed down out of the truck and Whitney noticed the pistol and holster slung over his shoulder.

"I think we have," he agreed. "As long as you don't call me Mr. Jones anymore."

"I see you cheated and took your revolver off again," she said.

He looked at her, surprised that she'd remembered his saying that and surprised even more that she noticed now. "I've had a fairly peaceful day. Not even one little shoot out," he teased.

They began walking toward the house. Rebel stood waiting on the porch, wagging his tail.

Whitney said, "My day was very peaceful, too. Pearl made me lie down and I ended up sleeping away the afternoon."

"Pearl knows what's good for a body." He opened the door and allowed her to enter before him.

Once they were inside, Whitney felt embarrassed. He'd probably thought she'd been sitting out on the steps waiting for him to come home just like an eager little wife. But the truth was she'd never waited on any man before.

He pulled off his gray Stetson and hung it on the hall tree. As he placed the pistol on the desk, he said, "But I'm surprised you listened to Pearl's advice."

Whitney shrugged as he turned back to face her. "I didn't know how to argue with her. I haven't had much dealings with old people."

Caleb reached up and pushed his fingers through his curly hair. In spite of his saying he'd had a quiet day, the gesture was that of a tired man. "Old people are just like young people," he said. "They just have a different wrapping."

He looked toward the kitchen. "Did Pearl cook anything?"

Whitney nodded. "Yes. But I don't know what she did with the leftovers."

Caleb unpinned the badge from his pocket, tossed it on the desk, then began to unbutton his shirt.

Whitney's eyes were drawn to his hands as they worked loose the buttons. They were long and lean, too, like the rest of his body. He wore no rings, but there was a gold watch with a black face on his left wrist. Whitney figured the only reason he had on the watch was because it was necessary to his job. He was not the jewelry-fancier type at all.

The last button on the shirt popped free and Whitney found herself swallowing, hoping he didn't intend taking it off in front of her, which she knew was ridiculous. She'd seen men without their shirts before, but not a man like Caleb. Somewhere between last night and now, she'd discovered he was good to look at. She didn't want to be tempted to look further.

"She'll have stowed them away somewhere," Caleb said. "I'll heat them for our supper as soon as I wash up."

He left the room and Whitney let out a pent-up breath. She didn't know what was wrong with her. Last night she'd looked at Caleb as someone standing in her way. Now she was seeing him as a man, a very masculine, sexy man.

It was a shocking realization for Whitney. She didn't look at men in a sexual or even romantic way. Certainly not since Edward, and even before him there hadn't been many men that had attracted her attention in that way. She couldn't understand why this one did.

Whitney went into the kitchen and found plates and silverware. She had the table set by the time Caleb appeared. He'd changed into a plain white T-shirt and the curls around his face were damp from his wash.

"Do you know how to cook, Whitney?"

Caleb went to the gas range where Pearl had placed the leftovers in foil-covered bowls. He lifted the cover on one, then smiled to himself when he discovered it was cabbage.

"I'm afraid I know nothing about cooking. I never learned."

He glanced over at her and Whitney felt insulted by the dry lift to his brows.

"I—I've had more important things to do," she felt compelled to say. "Besides, there's always the deli, or a restaurant. I'm not a big eater, anyway."

"Well," he drawled, beginning to remove the foil from the remaining bowls. "As you can see, there are no delis or eating places out here in the country. We have to do it ourselves."

Whitney rested the small of her back against the counter. "Personally, I don't know how you stand it."

"Stand what? The cooking, or the country living?"

Her lips curved with a wry smile. "Both, I suppose."

He reached down and took a saucepan from the bottom of the cabinet. Whitney watched his muscles bunch and flex beneath the thin T-shirt as he moved. Edward had never looked that way and he worked out in a gym at least twice a week. She took a deep breath and turned her eyes away from him.

"It's all what a person is accustomed to I suppose. If you took me to Manhattan and turned me loose, I'd be like a fish out of water. But that doesn't mean I wouldn't like it."

"Oh," she said with surprise. "Do you think you would like it? The city living, I mean."

He laughed just under his breath. "Maybe for a month. I doubt I could stand much more than that. But I think that's because I'm an outdoor person. I like to be in touch with the land, the wildlife and the elements. It's a part of me."

Yes, Whitney could see that. If he'd lived in a past era he'd probably have been a cowboy who'd roamed the Wild West, or a Dixie rebel fighting for his homeland.

"Now if I'd have been a banker or accountant, for instance," he went on, "New York would probably be a grand place to live."

Mulling over his words, Whitney walked across the kitchen and stood beside him as he warmed the food.

"What did you do today?" she asked curiously. "Drive around and let your presence be known?"

Caleb laughed at that. "A little." He looked over at her and was glad to see she'd calmed down since this morning. She wasn't smoking, she wasn't fidgeting, and she wasn't talking about leaving as though she were a fugitive on the run. Maybe there was a different side to this woman than he'd first thought.

He answered her. "Actually I had a run-in with an old friend. I had to fine him pretty heavily."

"You had to?"

He nodded, a grim expression on his face. "I had no choice. He was hunting out of season, without a license, and on private property to boot."

"Sounds like he was definitely asking for it."

"More like he was hungry. He has a family, several children and he's been out of work for nearly a year now. Venison, butchered and put away in the freezer, would be a big help on a grocery bill. But—" He stopped and shook his head at the hopelessness of it.

Whitney instinctively knew it had hurt him to apply the law in this instance. "It's not your fault that he's in financial trouble. You have a responsibility to do your job," she reasoned.

"Yes," he said with a sigh. "But that doesn't make it any easier for me to do. He'll never speak to me again. More than likely his wife or children won't, either."

Whitney watched him stir the cabbage. "But surely after he gets over his initial anger, he'll realize you were only doing your job."

Caleb's smile was rueful. "I doubt it. But there are laws to be obeyed, examples to be set. And because I'm the one enforcing them, I'm considered the tough guy without a heart. But when I took this job I knew there'd be repercussions.''

Whitney could have told him she knew all about repercussions. After all, they'd landed her here, with him.

Chapter Five

He finished warming the food and Whitney helped him carry it to the table. Caleb drank beer with his meal. Whitney settled for the raw milk, stirring down the cream and trying not to think of all the unhealthy fat she was consuming.

Once they finished eating, Whitney helped him wash the dishes. It was a job she'd never done before, but she discovered there was something soothing about methodically drying plates and glasses and placing them in the cupboard.

"Come outside with me," Caleb invited once the dishes were finished. He hung a wet dishtowel across a rack on the wall, then started toward the door. "You can help me feed General."

"And what is General?" Whitney asked, following him down the back porch steps. "Another bloodhound?"

Caleb laughed. "Rebel's not a bloodhound. He's a black-and-tan coonhound. General is a horse, a quarter

horse to be exact. Mine, more specifically. I use him to
check on my babies. In some places it's easier than a boat,
and quieter, too.''

"Your babies?"

They were walking across a small back lawn. Beyond a
board fence that separated the yard from the woods, there
was a small clearing. Whitney could see a faded red barn
some fifty yards to the left. Caleb headed in that direction.

"Alligators," Caleb informed her.

"Alligators! You must be joking. I thought those things
only lived in the Florida Everglades."

"No. Louisiana has them, too, living in the creeks and
the swamps. And I try to make sure these around here stay
safe and unharmed."

Caleb let out a shrill whistle and seconds later a big
brown horse with four white stockings trotted out of the
woods. Caleb walked up to him and affectionately hugged
the horse's neck. "Suppertime, ol' boy."

"You and Pearl certainly have a number of animals,"
she remarked, watching Caleb with the horse. He was obviously a man who respected life in all forms. The horse
was beautiful and obviously well cared for.

"It wouldn't be right to live in the country without animals. It would be sort of like going to a movie and not
eating popcorn."

Whitney smiled at his example. And then it suddenly
dawned on her that it had been a very long time since she'd
been to the theater and eaten popcorn. For the past few
months her father had harped over and over that her life
had narrowed down to one thing—work. She'd argued that
he was wrong. But for some reason Caleb was making her
look at things differently.

The two of them and the horse walked on to the barn. There was a small board corral annexed to it. General trotted inside the corral and sniffed impatiently at an empty feed trough built in one corner. Whitney stood outside the fence watching the beautiful animal as Caleb measured out grain into a galvanized bucket.

After a moment he appeared out of the shadows of the barn and handed the bucket to Whitney. "Here, I'll let you have the honors of feeding him while I get his hay. Just pour it in that trough over there." He nodded to where General was now impatiently pawing the earth.

Nodding, Whitney took the bucket from him and entered the corral. The horse crunched hungrily into the oats as soon as Whitney poured them.

After Caleb tossed fresh hay into a manger, the two walked slowly back to the house. The sun had gone down and the air was beginning to cool. Whitney tried to envision the weather in Manhattan, but it was difficult to do. For one thing, she'd never taken the time to notice the seasons' changes. She thought the leaves had begun to appear on the trees in Central Park, but she couldn't be sure.

Irritated at herself, she put those thoughts in the back of her mind and looked over at Caleb. "Who is Chester? Pearl mentioned something about him being angry if she didn't go home."

Caleb chuckled. "Chester is a black tomcat. He gets jealous when Pearl and Bernice, the calico, come over to my house."

"That's the craziest thing I've ever heard. Why doesn't he come, too?"

"Because Chester doesn't like me. I'm a male on his territory, therefore, I'm an enemy. Sometimes he'll come as close as the porch, if Pearl and Bernice stay too long.

Just to let out a few caterwauls and remind them to come home.''

Whitney shook her head in silent dismay. "Pearl mentioned her deceased husband. I forgot to ask her if she had children.''

"Unfortunately Pearl could never bear children. But she's everybody's grandmother and, I guess in a small way, that makes up for it.''

The phone was ringing when they entered the back door of the house. Caleb hurried to answer it while Whitney followed at a more leisurely pace.

In the living room she took a seat on the couch as Caleb propped a thigh over the corner of the desk and listened to the caller. After a moment he said in a patient voice, "I understand, Mrs. Johnson. And I promise I'll have a talk with the boy. I really don't think he's out to cause any harm." He paused, then continued, "No, I can't write him a fine unless one of my rangers, or myself, catch him at it.''

This brought Whitney's eyes over to Caleb. He looked at her and winked. The gesture brought a warm feeling to Whitney, as if he'd reached out and drawn her up next to him.

"Yes, I'll send a man out tomorrow, if it's not raining," he assured the woman. "Good evening, Mrs. Johnson.''

"An irate citizen?" she asked as he hung up the telephone.

Smiling, he shook his head. "Just a widow needing a little attention," he said. "Mrs. Johnson has a neighbor boy about twelve years old who sneaks over and fishes in her pond. She wants me to clap him in irons.''

"You people do take your fish seriously down here, don't you?" she asked dryly.

Caleb took a seat beside her and stretched his long legs out in front of him. He chuckled under his breath as he leaned his head back.

"When all was said and done, Mrs. Johnson would have a fit if I did anything to the boy. She just wants something to make a fuss about, and a reason to call me."

From the corner of her eye, Whitney looked over at him. "Oh, er, I guess she's one of those older women who find you irresistible?"

Amusement dimpled his cheek and crinkled the corners of his blue eyes. "Poor thing. It's not my fault. I can't help it that there's just so little of me to spread around."

"That is a sad thought," Whitney mocked, then asked, "Where did you get all that conceit?"

His head turned toward her. Whitney felt her breathing grow shallow as his wide grin showed white teeth beneath the gold-brown mustache.

"From my mama, I suppose. She was always telling me what a handsome boy I was. Still does."

Whitney looked away from him and swallowed. "She must be very proud of you."

Her voice was suddenly distant and the smile fell from Caleb's face as he watched a stiffness take hold of her features.

"Yeah, she and Daddy both are," he told her. "What about you, Whitney? I'll bet your mother was always telling you how pretty you were."

Whitney didn't know if he was complimenting her or merely making a comparison of their childhoods. Either choice disturbed her.

"Not really. She was always telling me I'd better do this or that if I ever expected to be pretty."

"Well, obviously it worked," he said. "You're a pretty woman."

Whitney darted her eyes over to him. Each time she'd thought he was going to dig into her, he'd surprised her with a simple but soothing remark. She felt very drawn to him and the feeling frightened her. She looked away from him once again and let out a tremulous breath. "Thank you for that," she said in a low voice.

Caleb was suddenly very still and very quiet. He had the unexplainable urge to kiss her. Not just the kind of kiss that comes from the lips, but the kind that comes from the heart. He didn't know why the feeling had come. But since it was a foreign one to him, he sat there for a moment examining it.

Night had settled over the Louisiana woods. The room was nearly dark now and outside the frogs and cicadas were orchestrating their own symphony. Whitney rose and walked over to the screen door. Staring out at the darkness, she breathed in the scent of the pines and asked pensively, "Are you always so happy, Caleb?"

He sat there looking at her tall, lovely form as he thought about her question. Happy? Of course he was happy. He didn't think a person should be anything but happy. It was the way God wanted a person to be.

Rising to his feet he walked up behind her. "Everyone has their down times, Whitney. But you'd be safe in writing my name down on the happy list."

She turned slightly and lifted her head up to his. There was a gentleness on his face, a tenderness in his eyes that Whitney had never encountered before. She couldn't believe that it was there for her.

"Why, Whitney? Aren't you happy?"

His question brought a knot of emotion to her throat. She swallowed and blinked, her eyes burning. For a long time she had viewed herself as a woman who had it all—a luxurious apartment, a successful career, a fiancé pledging to share the future with her. But now Caleb was making her wonder if she'd even been happy back then. Perhaps things hadn't been right for her even when she'd thought they were.

"I— Oh, Caleb," she said, choking. "I don't know what happy is anymore. Maybe...maybe I never knew."

He made a disapproving sound with his tongue, and then his hands were on her shoulders, drawing her toward him. Whitney knew that she should pull away, be strong and drag all her emotions back under control.

But for once Whitney didn't want to be in control. She wanted this strong man to hold her. She wanted to know what it was like to have her head cradled safely against his chest, to have his arms around her, comforting her, shielding her.

Without warning, tears fell onto her cheeks. Caleb stroked her hair and pressed her face against his shoulder.

"It's all right, Whitney," he murmured. "Everyone feels alone and afraid sometimes."

"It's more than that, Caleb. I—I've made a mess of everything, my life," she said tearfully.

His forefinger moved beneath her chin, drawing her face up to his. "I doubt that," he said with a seriousness that took her by surprise.

Whitney's tear-drenched eyes roamed over the lines and angles of his face until they finally settled on his mouth. A silent moment passed in which a warmth suddenly surged up inside her. It burned her cheeks as she whispered, "You can't say that, Caleb. You don't know me."

The corner of his mouth lifted to match the cocked arch of his brow. "No. But I'd like to," he said.

Before Whitney could reply, his lips were on hers, robbing her breath, searing her mind with the warmth of his kiss.

Long moments passed before Whitney realized she was clinging to him and that his hands had moved to her back, pulling her up tightly against him. And then the wall of hard muscle pressing into her shocked her senses back to awareness.

Whitney knew she should push away before things got out of hand, but his lips were warm and coaxing, producing a sweet fire that threatened to burst into flames. Frightened by her loss of control, Whitney pulled back from his embrace. Caleb reluctantly released his hold on her and watched as she turned her back to him.

She was shaking visibly and he wondered if he'd frightened her or, if like him, she'd been deeply affected by their kiss.

"Whitney, I—I didn't mean to frighten you," he said after a moment.

Gently he curved his hand over her shoulder. In response, Whitney swallowed and closed her eyes in a desperate attempt to ignore his touch.

"You . . . you didn't frighten me, Caleb," she replied in a low voice. "I just can't—" She turned around and forced out a short laugh. "I'm just not the kissing type."

Caleb could have argued that point. He'd felt the warmth, the need in her lips as they'd opened beneath his. But for some reason it was obvious she didn't want to acknowledge it to him or herself.

He let out a long breath and rubbed his thumb back and forth across her chin. She looked up at him and he was certain there was a faint mist in her dark eyes.

He smiled down at her. "Well, I definitely am the kissing type. So if you ever get the urge, just let me know."

Whitney saw the sparkle of warmth in his eyes and suddenly every nerve in her body sagged with relief. The whole thing had been just a lighthearted moment to him, nothing more. She had to think that was all it had been to her, too.

Dredging up another laugh, Whitney stepped around him and tossed the hair out of her eyes. She had to put some distance between them, even if it was only a matter of a few steps. "You're already spreading yourself thin, Caleb. I wouldn't want some little old lady whacking me over the head because I got the kiss that belonged to her."

Caleb wanted to tell her it had been a long time since he'd done any kissing, particularly any serious kissing. But he somehow knew she wouldn't want to hear it. It was obvious she wanted to treat the whole thing as a minor incident to be forgotten.

He suddenly wondered if there was a man in her life. And if that was what had really put her on the road. Caleb opened his mouth to ask, then abruptly decided it was too soon to be asking her anything that personal. She was like a flighty, nervous doe. The least little thing might scare her off, and that wasn't what he wanted to do.

"I don't think my little old ladies are really all that jealous," he teased.

Whitney turned to look at him. The room seemed smaller than it actually was as her eyes glided over him. In her mind they were still touching, still kissing.

"I—I think I'll sit out on the front porch," she said suddenly.

"Good idea," he returned. "I'll get a beer and join you. Want one?" he asked, starting off toward the kitchen.

"No, thank you," she answered before pushing through the screen door.

There were three webbed lawn chairs placed at the far end of the porch, but Whitney chose to sit on the planked boards with her feet resting on the top step. In just a moment Caleb stepped out of the house carrying a bottled beer. Without asking permission, he sat down beside her and twisted off the cap on the bottle.

Whitney stared out into the darkness, wondering why she felt the constant urge to drag in a deep breath. Her hands were still trembling and deep inside, she felt shaky and weak. Why had she gotten so lost in this man's arms? Why had it felt so good to touch him, to kiss him? For God's sake, she didn't even know him. She'd known Edward for a year and a half before they got engaged and he'd never affected her like this.

The questions were battling inside Whitney's head as Caleb spoke, breaking the silence. "It's a beautiful night. I don't suppose you can sit out like this back in Manhattan."

He stretched his long legs out in front of him and Whitney studied the rounded toes of his cowboy boots.

"No, I don't have a porch, or even a balcony. I wouldn't have time to sit on it even if I did," she said.

"Oooh, that's bad," he drawled in a disapproving tone. "You know, Whitney, there are two things that every house here in the South is required to have."

Curious now, she looked at him. "What's that?"

"A porch and a Bible."

A moment passed before she said, "Caleb, you're teasing now."

His teeth flashed in the twilight as he smiled at her. "It's a partial truth. You gotta have those things to be contented in life. Faith and relaxation. We Southerners know that."

Whitney looked across the way to where the lights from Pearl's house twinkled at the night.

"But how do you relax, Caleb, when your job and family are making demands? How do you hold on to your faith when you lose your job, your—" She broke off, wishing she hadn't spoken so much. Caleb seemed to do that to her, make her say far more than she'd ever said to anyone back home. "Well, you know what I mean."

He glanced over at her. There was a strained look on her face. Caleb decided there must be all kinds of pain bottled up inside her. He wished she felt close enough to share it with him.

"Good things come to those who are patient. Behind every sorrow there is a golden cloud. We have to believe that."

There was a genuine conviction in his tone that touched Whitney. Her voice was tinged with sadness when she spoke. "I lost my belief in rainbows when I was a child. Maybe it had something to do with my parents teaching that good things come to those who work and strive."

He leaned back and lazily propped himself up on his elbows. "Work is only one reason we're put on earth."

"And I'm sure you know the other reasons," she said dryly.

"Dancing, singing, eating, playing, laughing. Loving. You should try it sometime, Whitney. Life is fun."

Yes, she could see that life was fun for Caleb Jones. And she wished that it could be that easy, that simple for her.

His mouth quirked with impatience. "Are you broke?"

She looked down at him, her eyes widening as though she found his question ridiculous. "Not hardly!"

Whitney didn't want to sound snobbish, so she didn't go on to tell him that if she lived sensibly she had enough in trust funds to last into her old age. Besides, she had the distinct impression that Caleb didn't give a hoot about money.

"Then what the hell are you worried about?" he asked.

His question both stunned and angered her. "I'm not!"

"Could have fooled me," he countered before taking a swig of his beer.

Whitney's teeth ground together. The man obviously didn't understand her. "My job wasn't important to me solely for financial reasons."

"In other words, you liked what you did," he said, his blue eyes calmly watching the agitated thrust of her hands through her hair.

Caleb's statement caught her off guard. Her head twisted around and for a moment she merely stared at him. Her job had meant everything to her, but she'd never stopped to ask herself if she actually liked the work itself. It irritated her to think this man was presenting questions about her own life that she'd never taken the time to consider.

"Well, I guess I liked it. I was good at what I did," she told him, then turned her face back in the direction of Pearl's house, away from his prying eyes.

"What did you do back in Manhattan? Let me guess. You were an interior decorator?"

Whitney shook her head.

"Well, since you have a fixation with money, you must have been a loan officer in a bank."

Because she knew he was teasing, a smile crept across her face. "No."

"I know!" he said with a sudden snap of his fingers. "You were a broadway dancer."

"Caleb, really! Do I look theatrical?"

"You have long legs," he reasoned, and suddenly Whitney was laughing.

The sound was deep and rich. It was like music to Caleb's ears.

"You should do that more often you know," he told her once her laughter died away.

The smile fell from Whitney's face. "So I've been told," she said, all humor now gone from her voice. She was suddenly remembering her father telling her that she'd forgotten how to laugh.

At the time she'd thought he was merely trying to find fault with her. Especially since they'd been going around and around with each other over a particular magazine ad. But now she wondered if maybe her father had been pointing out the truth.

"Well, since you're not a dancer, I give up. What was your job?"

Whitney decided there wasn't any need to keep her job a secret. "I worked in advertising."

"Sounds impressive. What part did you play?"

He raised himself to a sitting position just in time to see a whimsical smile lift the corner of Whitney's lips. "I played the part of a boss—over the art department."

Caleb's brows peaked with interest. "A woman executive. My, my. And to think I kissed you."

Her cheeks burning, she darted him a confused glance. "What does that mean?"

"Well, I've heard ladies like you are sharks. I could have been bitten!"

Caleb knew he'd said the wrong thing from the sudden wounded look on her face. He reached out quickly to touch her arm, but before he could she was on her feet, rushing into the house.

Angry at himself, he also got to his feet and went inside. Whitney was nowhere to be seen. Instinctively he started toward the bedroom. The door was shut, and he knew without bothering to try the knob that it was also locked.

He let out an impatient breath. "Whitney, I'm sorry," he said. "I was only teasing."

There was no response. Caleb raked a hand through his hair and tried again. "You're not a shark. It was a joke. I can't help it if I have bad taste."

Still no response.

"Whitney," he said softly. "Don't be angry at me. The kiss was...was real nice. The nicest I can ever remember."

Behind the door, Whitney grabbed a pillow off the bed and buried her face in it. She couldn't let him hear her sobs. He thought she was angry and she wanted him to keep on thinking she was angry. That would be much easier than trying to explain to him the hurt in her heart.

"Come out and slap me or kick me," he invited. "It'll make us both feel a whole lot better."

His words brought a fresh burst of tears because kicking or slapping him was the last thing Whitney wanted.

The realization kept her behind the locked door for the remainder of the evening and throughout the long night.

Chapter Six

The next morning when Whitney opened the bedroom door, she stepped out with a suitcase in each hand. She glanced furtively toward the living room. Caleb was not in sight. She then looked the other way and her mouth promptly fell open.

Caleb was standing at the bathroom sink, wearing nothing but a pair of jeans and shaving cream on his face. As his eyes spotted her reflection in the mirror, the hand with the razor poised just above his jaw.

"Good morning, Whitney," he said cheerfully.

"Good morning," she replied coolly.

He turned around to look at her. "What are you doing?" he asked, his eyes going to her cases.

She grimaced. "I'd like for you to take me into Natchitoches today."

Quickly he stepped out of the bathroom to stand in front of her. Behind the shaving cream, there was a horrified expression on his face.

"Oh, Whitney, no! You don't want to do that. Are you still mad at me?"

From the sound of his voice, Whitney got the impression he wasn't used to a woman being angry with him at all, much less for any length of time. She didn't know whether to groan or weep. "I—I just—"

He broke in before she could go on. "Whitney, I'm truly sorry." He reached down, took the cases from her one by one and set them just inside the door of her room. "My best friend, Elliot, always did say my mouth was my own worst enemy. Don't leave just because I popped it off."

She took a deep breath and realized the pain that was in her chest last night was still there. Looking up at him, she said, "I think it's better that I leave. We're different people, we don't understand each other, and I don't belong here."

A rueful look twisted his mouth and dimmed the usual twinkle in his eyes. "You're still mad at me. You're mad about the kiss and—" His hands reached out and clasped her slender shoulders. "Whitney, I know you're not a shark," he said gently, his head lowering down to hers. "The kiss was sweet, soft. Let's do it all over again and you'll see."

Mesmerized, Whitney could only stare up at him with wide eyes. "Caleb, this . . . your . . ." She was so flustered by his closeness that she couldn't manage to put a coherent sentence together.

Thinking her hesitancy was because of the shaving cream on his face, Caleb grabbed the towel that had been tossed over his bare shoulder, and began to quickly wipe off his face, saying, "Oh, just a minute."

Before Whitney could dodge or utter a protest, his head swooped down. As soon as his lips touched hers, Whitney was at a complete loss. His jaws were still moist and scented from the shaving cream. The parts of skin he'd shaven were smooth, the other parts rough. The contrast was strangely erotic as he rubbed his face against hers.

Groaning, she reached her hands out blindly for support. The first thing they came in contact with was his hard midsection. Her fingers flattened against the warm skin above his jeans as his mouth continued its gentle search of hers.

When his head finally lifted, Whitney's legs were weak and trembling, her eyes half-closed. Caleb's hand came up and touched the skin of her throat, her cheek and finally moved to her hair.

"You're just about the softest thing I've been around in a long time. Nothing like a shark," he said with a sensual grin and a glint in his blue eyes. "No sharp teeth, no snapping jaws. Just soft, pale skin, and dark wavy hair."

His finger wound itself through a strand, his forehead leaned into hers. "You *are* going to forgive me, aren't you? You aren't going to make me suffer for the rest of my life over one little slip of the tongue, are you?"

Whitney knew he was trying to charm her into staying. She didn't stop to ask herself why he was doing it; she only knew she had to fight this sudden attraction she felt for him. But being close to him, with his mouth only a fraction away from hers, made it hard. Very hard.

"I'm not...angry about the kiss," she finally managed to say.

"That's good," he drawled huskily, and smiled at her.

Whitney swallowed uncomfortably. "But I still want to leave," she said.

His face wrinkled with confusion. "Now, Whitney, that just doesn't make any sense at all."

Before her determination crumbled, Whitney turned around and grabbed her cases. "It never really made any sense for me to stay here," she said, her back turned to him. "I appreciate all you've done for me. But now it's time for me to leave. I'm sure once I'm gone you'll be relieved not to have the burden of a houseguest."

Caleb frowned helplessly as he watched her lift the cases. He didn't want her to go. Already he liked having her around. He wanted to keep her around.

"You're not a houseguest. You're my friend."

The way he said "friend" shot a tiny arrow of pain through Whitney because she knew Caleb was a man who didn't take the word lightly.

She turned around to face him. "Thank you, Caleb. That's very nice of you. But I'm really determined to go this time."

Caleb shrugged resignedly and stepped out of her way. "Then I guess I'll just have to respect your wishes. We'll leave after breakfast, okay?"

Whitney couldn't understand why there was a lump in her throat, or why it was so hard to meet his blue eyes. "Yes, that will be fine."

She was doing the right thing, Whitney told herself a few minutes later as she placed her last case in the back of Caleb's pickup. She couldn't let this man affect her life. She couldn't let herself become attracted to a stranger. He wasn't from her world, and she wasn't from his. She'd already had one disastrous encounter with a man. She wasn't going to take the risk of having another.

Caleb cooked pancakes and sausages for their breakfast. Whitney set the table, but otherwise stayed out of his way as he moved around the small confines of the kitchen.

In a matter of minutes Caleb had the meal ready and they were eating.

"It's going to be another beautiful day," Caleb remarked as he sliced the stack of pancakes on his plate.

Whitney sipped her coffee and directed her gaze outside the window. The sun was just rising and the yard was filled with bird song. From the open window she could smell the dew and the scent of the pines, and see a giant azalea bush that was covered with snow-white blossoms.

"Yes, beautiful," she replied, unaware of the wistful note in her voice.

"If you were back in New York at this moment what would you be doing?"

She turned her eyes back to him, letting them roam over the handsome appearance he made sitting across from her. The uniform and the badge suited him. He was not just a man who looked good—he was also a good man. Authority, honor and decency were carved into the strong lines of his face.

In spite of everything, Whitney was glad their lives had crossed in this small way. She would always remember Caleb, his smile, his laugh, the tender mystery of his kiss.

"You mean if I were still working?" she asked, forcing her mind to deal with his question.

He nodded and she went on. "Oh, I'd be rushing around my apartment, dressing and trying to remember what kind of day my secretary had scheduled for me."

"No breakfast?"

Whitney smiled ruefully as she glanced down at her plate. "Not like this. Maybe a quick glass of orange juice, or a Danish on the way to work."

With his eyes still on her face, he smiled and reached for his coffee. "That's bad and that's good."

Whitney threw him a questioning glance and he said, "Bad that you don't take time to eat a proper breakfast.

Good that you don't have a man like me cooking one for you.''

She let out a shaky laugh as she stabbed her fork into the pancakes. His direct gaze bothered her, his nearness bothered her, the memory of his kiss bothered her. Leaving this place and him behind was the only way to get him out of her life.

''Believe me, Caleb, there are no men like you back in New York,'' she said, forcing her voice to be light. ''Besides, my housekeeper/cook is a woman.''

Her words produced a laugh from Caleb. Whitney kept her eyes on her plate and tried to fight off the depression that was creeping over her like a dark, heavy fog.

Once they finished breakfast Caleb insisted he didn't have time to bother with the dishes. Whitney was relieved. She didn't want to spend any more time with him than necessary. Time with Caleb was temptation and in her vulnerable state of mind, she needed to be out of temptation's reach.

The early morning air was cool and pleasant when the two of them eventually walked outside to the pickup. Rebel followed at Caleb's heels, then sat back on his haunches and whined as the two humans climbed into the vehicle.

''Are you sure you don't want to say goodbye to Pearl? She'll be hurt, you leaving like this without a word.''

Whitney shook her head. ''It's too early to disturb her. Besides, I'm certain it won't matter to Pearl if I'm gone. The woman hardly knows me.''

Caleb shook his head as though he didn't understand her reasoning. ''Whatever you say,'' he said, glancing across the seat at her as he guided the truck down the dirt lane.

She was wearing a sundress with skinny little straps. It was pink and he could tell just by looking at it that the dress was expensive, just like the slacks and blouse she'd had on yesterday. She was a beautiful enigma to him, one that he wanted more than anything to unravel. He knew that somewhere between here and the twenty-five miles to Natchitoches he had to think of some way to keep her with him.

"You know, there's lots of things you need to see while you're in Natchitoches," he told her as the pickup rattled over the rough road. "Like several old plantations. And I'd bet you'd love a trip down the river, with the lights from town twinkling down on the water like stars. I'd be an excellent guide."

Whitney grabbed her purse and fished out a cigarette. After she'd lit it and blew out a wreath of smoke, she said, "I'll take a walk around town. It'll be enough for me."

"But that's a shame! I can't let you go off to Texas without first seeing Louisiana."

Whitney puffed on her cigarette. "I'm not on a sight-seeing tour, Caleb. I'm on this trip for time alone."

She'd never told him why she needed that time alone. He figured it was somehow connected to her job and her father. He felt inclined to ask her now, but decided not to. Keeping her around was the most pressing issue at the moment. "Well, like I told you before, you need to stop and smell the flowers along the way," he pointed out, reaching up and tugging his hat further down on his forehead. "And I'm a good flower-smeller, too."

Whitney flicked her ashes in the ashtray on the dashboard, then looked over at him, a tiny smile creeping across her face. She couldn't help but smile at him. He made her smile with his humor, his warmth and concern, the flirty glint in his eyes. Edward hadn't possessed a fraction of this man's charm. Her friends back home might call it uncultivated charm, but then they wouldn't understand Caleb any better than they had understood her, she reasoned with her thoughts.

They passed the spot where Whitney had wrecked the Jaguar. After that it was only a couple of minutes before they reached the main highway, and Caleb turned east. Five miles or more had passed when Mabel's voice crackled out on the two-way radio.

"Caleb, you there?"

Caleb reached for the mike. "Right here, Mabel. What's going on this morning? You got a pot of coffee made for me, yet?"

"You'll have to wait on the coffee this morning, Caleb. The sheriff up in Red River Parish just called. He needs you, pronto. They got a little hunt going up there. You might want to bring Rebel."

"I'll get right up there, Mabel. Radio the sheriff and tell him I'll be there as soon as I can."

"Will do," Mabel's voice came back.

The next instant Caleb made a sharp U-turn in the middle of the highway.

Wide-eyed, Whitney clung to the dashboard. "What's the matter? Where are we going?"

"Home," he said, his attitude suddenly all business. "I have to get Rebel and it looks like you'll have to stay here another night. I don't have time to take you into Natchitoches now."

"But—" she began desperately, only to have him shake his head at her.

"This is an emergency, Whitney. I'm sorry."

She sank helplessly back against the seat. "What...what did she mean by a 'hunt'? What are they hunting? Doesn't that sheriff have deputies?"

Caleb stepped down hard on the gas pedal, sending them flying down the narrow highway. "Of course, he has deputies. But I know the swamps and bayous around there. They're probably going to flush out some poachers or stillers. Nothing dangerous," he said in a dismissive way.

The dirt road leading back was rough, yet Caleb didn't slacken the truck's speed. Whitney felt shaken to pieces by the time he braked to a quick halt in front of the house.

He was on the ground, strapping the pistol to his hip and whistling for Rebel by the time Whitney gathered up her handbag and climbed down out of the seat. The hound appeared almost instantly and Whitney stood to one side as Caleb quickly let down the tailgate so that the dog could jump up into the truck bed. She looked from Caleb, with the gun on his hip, to the dog, then back to Caleb.

"When will you be back?" she asked, sensing his urgency to be on his way.

"Whenever the job gets done. Remember, Pearl's here if you need anything."

"Yes, well, it looks as though I have no choice in the matter," she said, feeling very helpless and uncertain.

Caleb quickly climbed behind the steering wheel, slammed the door shut, then looked at her out the open window.

"'Bye, Whitney."

"Goodbye, Caleb."

With a smile and a quick salute from the brim of his Stetson, he gunned the pickup down the road.

Whitney stood in the yard and watched until the dust had cleared away and Caleb was out of sight.

By noon Whitney was pacing the floors, and she couldn't understand why. After Caleb had left this morning, the only thing she'd had on her mind was his coming back, so that she could finally leave this place once and for all. But now as the hours passed all she could think about was Caleb coming home, period.

Whitney stared out the front screen door, her mind racing. Mabel had said there was a hunt going on. What did that mean? she wondered, irritated. If the people around here would use English instead of colloquialisms she might understand what was going on.

The woods around Caleb's and Pearl's houses were silent except for the birds, and the quiet grated on Whitney's nerves. The stillness allowed her to think more than she wanted to think.

Pressing her nose against the screen, she let out a restless breath. Was Caleb in danger? He'd said not. But he'd strapped his pistol on with such swift determination that she was inclined to think otherwise. He'd taken Rebel, and even though he'd told her that the dog wasn't a bloodhound, she supposed he was a hunting dog of sorts. And what would a law officer need with a hunting dog unless he was hunting criminals?

The whole idea frightened Whitney. Then she told herself it was silly of her to be afraid for someone she didn't even know. Caleb was just a man who'd given her a place to stay for the past couple of days, that was all. What he did on the job was no concern of hers.

By one o'clock Whitney was walking across the lawn toward Pearl's house. She'd paced, smoked, sat and paced again until she could stand it no longer. If she didn't hear the sound of another human being's voice soon she was going to scream.

Pearl was sitting on the front porch in an old oak rocking chair with a woven rope bottom. Chester and Bernice, oblivious to the creak of the chair, were asleep at her feet. In Pearl's lap was some sort of bright-colored, patchworked material.

"Hello, Whitney," the old woman spoke as she jabbed a small, shiny needle down into the material and pushed it through with a thimbled thumb. "What are you up to today?"

Whitney sank down on the edge of the porch and looked up at the woman. "I'm still stranded. Caleb was going to take me into Natchitoches today, but he was called out on an emergency."

"Yes. I knew that."

Surprised, Whitney studied Pearl's softly wrinkled face. "You did?"

"I saw you loading your suitcases this morning. Then I saw you coming back. I turned on the scanner and heard Caleb talking."

Whitney latched onto to one word. "Scanner? You mean one of those police scanners?"

Pearl nodded as she continued sewing. "Caleb got it for me so I could hear the storm warnings. He doesn't like to leave me back here alone when the weather is ripe for a tornado."

That sounded like Caleb, Whitney thought, then wondered how many other young men would take time to care for an elderly widow woman.

"So," Whitney asked, moistening her lips. "What did you hear this morning?"

Pearl muttered something under her breath, then shook her head and reached down in her lap for a pair of wire-framed glasses. She perched them on the end of her nose and took another jab with her needle. "Damn spectacles, they're as bothersome as a fly."

Whitney placed a hand over her forehead and told herself to be patient. People around here went at a slow pace. She wasn't in the hustle and bustle of her Manhattan office.

"Sounded like they had a couple of escapees penned in a swamp up there in Red River Parish. Came down from a work facility in Arkansas, I think."

Fear shot through Whitney like a jagged streak of lightning. "What kind of escapees?"

Pearl shrugged one small shoulder. "Don't know. Did hear they had guns on them, though."

Whitney swallowed as her throat and mouth went suddenly dry. "Guns! And Caleb's up there now trying to track them down?"

Pearl held out her handiwork for a closer examination. "He'll track them down," she said with certainty. "Caleb's been shot at before. He's not afraid of meeting up with a bullet."

Whitney couldn't believe how casually the old woman was viewing the whole situation. "In New York, where I live, policemen are often killed," she told Pearl, fear threading through her voice.

Pearl's lips pursed to a thoughtful line. "I expect that's true enough. But you're not in New York now, Whitney. Do you good to remember that."

Whitney let out a deep sigh. After a moment Pearl leaned forward in the rocker and patted Whitney's head. "You're worried about Caleb, aren't you?"

Whitney had to admit that she was worried. Very worried. She nodded, her face glum. "Yes, I guess I am."

Pearl clucked her tongue. "No need for that, girl. Caleb's been in this business for a long time. He's good at it. So tell me, how come you were going to leave this morning? Yesterday after that fainting spell you had, you were all ready to stay for a while."

Blushing, Whitney looked away from Pearl and out across the green lawn with its stand of pines and bright azalea bushes. "I—I just decided I was in the way. I didn't want to impose any longer."

"Hmm," Pearl commented, adjusting the glasses on her nose once again. "I don't think Caleb saw you as an imposition. But I guess you saw things that way, guess you have your own life to get on with anyway."

Whitney nodded her head jerkily. "Yes. Yes, I do."

Pearl took a few more stitches. "I guess you were going to tell Caleb goodbye and never see him again."

Whitney looked back at Pearl. What was the old woman getting at? What was she expecting her to say? "Well, yes. I suppose that was the way it would have been. I doubt I'll ever be back this way again, so there wouldn't be a chance to see Caleb again."

Pearl cocked an eyebrow upward as she peered over the rim of her glasses at Whitney. "Then why are you fretting about him? If you were planning on leaving and not seeing him again anyway, it shouldn't matter to you what he's doing about now."

As Pearl's words sunk in, Whitney made a helpless gesture with her hands. "I— Caleb is a fellow human being. I wouldn't want anything to happen to him, just like I wouldn't want anything to happen to you or anyone else."

"Oh, I see."

It was all the old woman said and after several moments passed Whitney felt her shoulders slumping. She wasn't being totally honest with Pearl. Caleb was more than just a fellow human being. He was special. He'd been special from the moment she'd first met him that night in the rain. Thinking of never seeing him again left her with a strange, hollow feeling.

Caleb was so full of life. There was no pretense about him and Whitney liked that. His smile was warm and contagious and he laughed more than anyone she knew. He made her feel better without even trying, and just looking at him made her aware of herself as a woman. No man had ever done that to her.

The admission scared her, but she had to face it. She'd run from her problems in New York. She decided she didn't want to run from Caleb, too.

"Pearl, what do you think makes a woman a woman?"

Pearl dropped her sewing to look at Whitney's pensive face. "That depends," she said.

Whitney shrugged. "I think . . . things are so different now from what they were when you, or even my mother, was a young woman. Now women are supposed to be everything. Smart, independent, creative, sexy, beautiful, dedicated mothers and wives, with a fulfilling career on the side. Is that the way you see things?"

"Maybe you're asking the wrong person, dear. I'm a simple person. But I do feel like a woman, even though I'm an old one now." She picked up her sewing once again. "I think just following the feelings in our hearts is what makes us the man or woman we are, not following a set of rules."

Whitney was inclined to agree. But how did you go about doing that when the outside world was coming at you from all directions?

She looked up at Pearl and smiled faintly. Today, the old woman was wearing a purple printed dress with short sleeves and a rounded neck. Tiny little onyx earrings dangled from her ears and her black hair was pinned to her head in a braided coronet. She was beautiful in spite of her age, and it was easy for Whitney to imagine Pearl young and in love with her husband, Ben.

"Yes, I think you're right, Pearl. It's just . . . hard to do sometimes."

Whitney leaned over and scratched Bernice between the ears, while wishing she could quit thinking about Caleb. She hoped with everything inside her that he was safe. She wanted more than anything to see him driving up in his truck, safe and sound. She realized with a great deal of surprise that she yearned for that much more than she wished to be gone, wished to get her car back, even wished to have her job back.

Scooting closer to Pearl's knee, she studied the woman's handiwork. "What are you making?" she asked in hopes of diverting her troubled thoughts.

"A quilt. This is the top part."

"And you do all that by hand? The pieces are so tiny! Couldn't you use a sewing machine?"

"Suppose so," Pearl mused, "but it wouldn't look as pretty. It wouldn't mean as much to me once I finished it, either."

It was obvious that Pearl had pride in her work. For a long time Whitney had thought she'd had pride in her job, too. But now that she'd been away from it, she was beginning to take a second look. True, she'd put everything she'd had into her job. But she'd done it to make money for the agency, to prove to her father that she was worthy of the job. That wasn't quite the same as giving it your pride.

"Will it be some sort of specific design?"

Pearl spread the square across her lap to give Whitney a better look. "This is called a double wedding ring pattern. Once all the pieces are sewn together, two circles will be entwined in the middle. It's an old, old pattern."

"It sounds lovely," Whitney said.

"Here, why don't you try a few stitches?" Pearl said, handing down the needle to Whitney.

Whitney quickly shook her head. "I've never sewn anything in my life. I don't want to make a mess of your work."

Pearl quickly rose from the rocker and motioned for Whitney to follow her. "Well, come along, then, and I'll give you something to keep your hands busy, and your mind off Caleb."

Whitney got to her feet and followed the old woman into the house.

Chapter Seven

Whitney stayed the remainder of the day at Pearl's house. The woman put her to work cutting out tiny pieces of printed fabric for the quilt. Throughout the afternoon Pearl talked of how her Cajun mother had married a riverboat gambler in Natchez. He'd gotten into some sort of skirmish with the law and in order to avoid prosecution they'd fled to Louisiana, where they'd eventually settled for life.

It was an interesting story and Whitney listened intently, grateful for anything to pull her thoughts away from Caleb if only for a few minutes at a time.

When evening approached, Pearl cooked a supper of pork chops and boiled poke salad scrambled with eggs. The food was delicious but after so long without a word from Caleb, Whitney's worry had returned and ruined her appetite.

Pearl decided to turn on the police scanner to see if they could hear anything concerning the hunt, but all that was being reported was a car wreck somewhere in Sabine Parish, and a kitchen fire in someone's house. After a while Whitney gave up and walked back to Caleb's house. It seemed as quiet as a tomb when she entered the front door. Not knowing what else to do, she forced herself to turn on the television and settle down to watch it.

By eleven o'clock she decided there was no use in waiting up any longer. It could be hours before Caleb returned home.

She took a long shower and washed her hair. Since her cases were still in the back of Caleb's pickup, she found one of his shirts in the closet and used it for a nightshirt. It was made of blue cotton and hung to her mid-thighs. The sleeves went past her fingertips and she rolled them up to her elbows before she climbed into bed.

It was past one when Caleb drove up in front of the house and shut off the motor and lights. Rebel lay exhausted on the floor. Caleb went around to open the door and coax the dog out.

"We're home, ol' boy. You can rest now."

The hound jumped to the ground and followed Caleb onto the porch. Rebel immediately flopped down and stretched out on his side. He was covered with mud, and so was Caleb.

The house was dark and quiet. Caleb made no sound as he walked across the living room and headed down the small hallway that led to the bedrooms. When he reached Whitney's he stopped in the open doorway and looked in.

It was special for Caleb to see her there, lying on her side, her black hair spread out on the pillow. He'd never thought of coming home to a woman before, until today. And unexpectedly, he wished he had the right to cross the room and gently wake her, take her in his arms and kiss her.

But Caleb doubted she'd be receptive to that kind of greeting. Hell, he thought with a grimace, she'd probably get mad all over again and demand that he drive her into Natchitoches tonight.

That sobering thought sent him to the bathroom, where he flipped on the light and proceeded to wash some of the mud from his face and hands. Then he left the house to feed his horse.

Whitney woke suddenly. Seeing the light on in the bathroom, she jumped from the bed, expecting to find Caleb there.

"Caleb? Where are you?" she called.

There was no immediate answer. She began to walk through the house in search of him when a noise sounded at the back door. Whitney hurried out to the kitchen just in time to see him coming in.

She went still as her eyes took in the sight of him. His jeans were wet and muddy, as were his boots. His shirt wasn't in much better shape and there were flecks of mud plastered to his gray Stetson. He looked tired, but as his eyes met hers across the room a smile spread across his face.

"So you woke up," he said.

"Yes, I saw your light. I wanted to make sure you were all right."

Whitney's warm words sent some of the tiredness away from his weary body. Reaching up, he removed his hat, tossed it on the counter, then ran both hands through his hair. Looking back at her, he smiled again. "I'm fine," he assured her. "Just tired."

Whitney was so glad to see him that all she could manage to do was stand there and look at him.

He asked, "Did you have anything left over from supper to eat?"

"Er, I ate over at Pearl's," she said, forcing her body to move into action. "But maybe I could gather you something together. Why don't you sit down? You look exhausted."

Caleb's eyes ran over her bare legs and feet beneath his shirt as she opened the cabinets. He was exhausted but the sight of Whitney's white skin was doing strange things to him.

"I thought you didn't know how to cook," he said as he sank gratefully into a chair at the kitchen table.

"I'll manage something," she said. "Just tell me what happened."

Since she was concentrating on the meal, Caleb allowed his eyes to follow each and every movement she made.

"We got the job done," he told her with a negligible shrug. "Two convicts. They'd been loose for three days after jumping a couple of guards while out on a work patrol. They swore not to be taken alive, but when they were faced with a pack of hounds and the end of a few shotgun barrels they had a change of heart."

"Well," she said, sighing with great relief, "I'm sure you're glad to get that job over with. Uh, were there any shots fired?"

Caleb ran his eyes up to her face, wondering if maybe she had been worried about him. It would be nice to know she had been. Not really worried, he thought, but maybe just a little worried.

"A few," he said. "How did you know they were armed?"

"Pearl," she answered. "She heard it on the scanner this morning."

His smile was wry. "Pearl hears things on that scanner that she shouldn't hear."

"She says you got it for her," Whitney reasoned.

"That was only for weather reasons. Pearl would sit in her rocker and let the porch crash in on her head if I didn't make her go to the cellar. But to answer your question, yes, there were a few shots fired. They were harmless ones though."

Whitney would never view a fired bullet as harmless. It made her realize how thankful she was to have him back home. "It would make me furious to have someone shoot at me," she said. "Not to mention that it would frighten me out of my mind."

Caleb chuckled. "What made me more furious was having to trudge at least ten miles through the swamps chasing them down. I'd rather get my exercise some other way."

Whitney walked over to the table to place a plate of sardines, crackers, cheese and sliced tomatoes in front of him. Beside the plate she set a jar of mustard.

Surprise marked his face as he looked at the fare. "Oh, darlin', aren't you sweet."

Whitney blushed at the compliment and the endearment. "Just a minute and I'll get you a beer and some silverware."

After she'd gotten him those two items, Whitney took the seat across from him. She folded her arms on the table as Caleb began to eat.

"I'm sorry about having to leave you this morning. I know you were determined to go and—"

Whitney held up her hand to stop the flow of his words. "Please, don't apologize. You have your job to do. Besides, I . . . I'm almost beginning to enjoy the quiet back here in this place."

His eyes remained on her face as he squashed a sardine between two crackers. "Grows on a person, doesn't it?"

She nodded and pushed her tangled hair out of her eyes. "I spent most of the day with Pearl. She's an interesting woman."

"I'm glad you like her," he said, then crunched into the sandwich he'd just made. He swallowed the bite, washed it down with a drink of beer, then added, "And I'm glad you weren't angry at me because I couldn't take you into Natchitoches."

Whitney felt a hesitant smile curve her lips. "I wasn't angry. I was worried. I'm glad you made it back home safely."

The grin on his face told Whitney he was pleased by her words. "You're a hard one to figure out, Whitney Drake."

"Why do you say that?"

"I never seem to know how you'll take things. For instance, the business about the shark. Whitney, I'm really sorry—"

"Forget it," she said quickly, her eyes dropping to the tabletop. "I was being overly defensive."

He didn't make a reply and Whitney forced herself to lift her eyes and meet his gaze.

"You see," she spoke again, her voice flat, "I've been more or less accused of being a shark before...by a man."

Oh, Lord, Caleb thought, no wonder she'd reacted so strongly to what he'd only meant as teasing. He'd really managed to put his foot in his mouth. "I take it the man was important to you?"

She took a deep breath, let it out, then looked across the kitchen. "He was my fiancé, Edward Glenbrough."

Everything inside Caleb went still for a moment, even the beating of his heart. "Was? Does that mean he isn't now?"

Whitney looked back at Caleb and nodded. There was a cold stiffness to her face that made him want to reach across the table and take her hand.

"He broke our engagement about two months before the wedding date."

"Because he thought you were a shark?" he asked, lifting the beer bottle to his lips again.

With a wry grimace Whitney thrust her fingers through her black hair. Caleb sat quietly watching her, wondering what was going through her mind, while at the same time thinking how beautiful she was. Her skin had the soft sheen of a pearl and her hair was shockingly dark against its ivory color. The darkness of her eyes also dramatized her features and he figured he was far from the first man to appreciate her beauty.

"I suppose you could put it that way. He said I'd become too business-oriented, that I loved my job and only my job and that he wanted a woman, not a business machine."

There was no mistaking the wounded look on her face. Caleb hated knowing that some other man had put it there. "And I'll bet you told him you didn't want a little pipsqueak like him hanging around waiting for a handout, either, didn't you?" he teased in an effort to lighten the moment and to see her smile again.

It took a moment or two, but finally her lips began to curve upward. "I suppose I should have. Edward really was a pipsqueak," she said with wry conviction.

"See how happy you should be? You had a narrow escape."

Her laugh was soft and a bit whimsical. "Yes, I suppose I did. Although I didn't think so at the time. It makes me angry at myself because I wasn't seeing things as they really were back at that time."

Caleb took his eyes off her long enough to make another sardine sandwich. Whitney watched his strong hands at work, then allowed her eyes to drift up to his face. She realized at that moment how much she liked being with Caleb. She'd never shared her real feelings over Edward's rejection with anyone. But it felt right to talk to Caleb about it. She instinctively felt that he would understand.

"And how did you see Edward, back when you weren't really seeing, that is?" Caleb asked once he was eating again.

Whitney waved her hand dismissively and leaned back in her chair. Caleb took the opportunity to let his eyes wander discreetly down the length of her crossed legs.

"I saw him as a smart, successful man in the clothing business. He had a long list of steady assets, he didn't drink, didn't smoke or swear." And marriage to Edward would have pleased her father. In fact, Edward had been his choice, not Whitney's.

"Hmm," Caleb said thoughtfully. "I guess I wouldn't fit on the standard husband list. I drink beer, and I say 'hell' and 'damn,' and the only smart I've been accused of being is smart-mouthed. As for my assets—well, let's just say they've been liquidated a long time ago."

A burst of laughter slipped past Whitney's lips. "Somehow I don't think you and Edward would value the same assets," she told him.

He grinned as he finished the food on his plate. "I doubt it. And as for you calling him smart, that obviously doesn't fit the man or he'd never have let you go."

Reaching across the table, Caleb took hold of her hand and squeezed it gently. "You're really much better off without him, Whitney," he murmured.

"Yes, I'm sure I am, too," she said, lifting her eyes to meet his. In fact, at this moment, Whitney was never more sure of anything in her life.

Awkward moments ticked by as Caleb continued to hold her hand. Yet Whitney couldn't bring herself to pull away. Her eyes clung to his face, noting the lines of fatigue beneath his eyes and around his mouth. She longed to lean forward and smooth them away with her fingers.

"You must be very tired," she finally managed to say. "Why don't you go on to bed and I'll clean this mess up for you."

He released her and pushed his chair back from the table. "You're right, I'm very tired," he agreed.

Whitney got to her feet and started gathering the dirty dishes. Caleb kept his seat, looking up at her as he casually said, "By the way, I have tomorrow off. I thought it would be a nice opportunity to take you sightseeing."

She stopped her work and glanced down at him. She wanted to be with him, but how could she let him know? Just this morning she'd insisted on leaving this place and him behind. Now leaving was the last thing she wanted. It didn't make sense to Whitney, so how could she possibly explain it to him?

"I— Do you think—"

He suddenly stood and Whitney was forced to crane her neck back to look at him.

"I know you've been cooped up here and that you're wanting to leave. But you don't want to spend the time waiting in a motel room while your Jaguar is being repaired. What do you say?"

She held up her hands in helpless response. "I'd say it's very hard to argue with you."

"Does that mean you'll stay?"

She felt her heart thump with a strange excitement as her gaze touched his lips and she remembered the feel of them. It was probably crazy and dangerous to stay in this man's company. But something made her want to take the risk.

"Yes, I suppose so," she answered.

"Good," he said with a broad smile, then added with a devilish wink, "because I've already brought your cases back in. You might as well know that I had no intentions of leaving you in Natchitoches this morning, either."

Before Whitney could say anything else, he turned and left the room, throwing a "goodnight" over his shoulder as he went.

Chapter Eight

It wasn't quite daybreak the next morning when Whitney woke to the smell of coffee and frying bacon. Quickly she threw on a thin, blue cotton robe and went to the kitchen.

Caleb was standing at the stove in a pair of jeans and a short-sleeved black polo shirt. His sandy-colored hair tumbled in wet curls about his head and there was an engaging smile on his face as he lifted his head to greet her.

"Good morning. Have a nice sleep?"

Whitney walked farther into the room, yawning behind her hand as she went. "You've only been in bed a few hours. You should have gotten more sleep."

He waved the spatula in an offhand gesture.

"It doesn't take much sleep for me. Are you hungry this morning?"

She folded her arms across her breasts as she stood beside him, eyeing the eggs and bacon in the skillet.

"I've never eaten breakfast before. Now for three mornings in a row I am. This place is doing something to me."

Caleb glanced over at her, remembering how nervous she'd been that first morning after he'd found her.

"That's good to hear. It means I must be doing something right."

She gave him a droll look. "I take it that means you think I needed to change?"

Caleb reached for a plate and began to ladle the eggs and bacon onto it. "I think when I found you in that wrecked car you were like a scared little rabbit. Even when you had a safe haven poked under your nose, you still wanted to run."

Whitney dropped her arms to her sides and took the plate he offered her.

"A rabbit," she mused aloud. "Well, I suppose that's an improvement over a shark. Do you always compare women to animals?"

Caleb chuckled as he followed her to the table. "Only if they make an impression on me."

Whitney wondered what kind of impression she'd made on him, but refrained from asking. It might not be wise to know what this man's real thoughts were.

They began to eat and much to Whitney's surprise she discovered she was hungry. Caleb had also made toast and hash browns. There was blackberry jam from Pearl and Whitney caught herself slathering a second piece of toast with the sweet concoction.

"I hope you didn't take a day off just for my benefit," she told him after a few moments. "It's not your responsibility to entertain me."

Smiling, he sipped his coffee. "I do take time off and yesterday was a hard day. Besides, the thought of 'entertaining' you is stuck in my mind. I won't be worth two cents if I don't spend this day with you."

Something about his words made her blush. He'd said them in a teasing tone, but still there was an underlying message in them.

Her eyes went across to him as she shook back her tangled black hair. "I suppose you have the whole day planned?"

He gave her a brief shake of his head. "I'm not a planner, just a doer. It's more fun that way, don't you think?"

Fun. When was the last time she'd thought about having fun? "I hadn't really thought about it," she answered truthfully.

He put down his empty coffee cup as he watched a frown pucker the space between her brows. "Well, don't look so worried, Whitney. Fun isn't painful. You'll like it once you get the hang of it. I promise."

Whitney felt a smile creep across her mouth. "You promise what? That I'll have fun, or it won't hurt?"

"Both," he chuckled. "Now go get dressed while I clean things up here."

Thirty minutes later they were traveling down the highway in Caleb's government pickup. The rifles were still hanging in the back window, but Whitney did her best to ignore them. The sun was shining brightly and Caleb had the radio tuned to a rock station.

"For a man who likes to take things slowly, why do you like rock music?" she asked.

He propped his right arm lazily against the back of the seat while keeping his left hand on the steering wheel. There was a naughty glint in his eyes when he looked over at her. "Well, Whitney, I don't like everything slow!"

She glossed over the implication of that and went on to say, "I figured you to be one of those country music guys. Heartbreaking, crying-in-your-beer-type stuff."

"Honey," he laughed, "if you try to figure me out too much you'll hurt yourself. Just sit back and look at the scenery—and at me. I'm almost as good looking, don't you think?"

Whitney groaned and shook her head. "I wouldn't tell you even if I thought you were. Your head would probably get so big you'd have to take off that Stetson you're wearing."

Caleb's eyes drifted up to the brim of his gray hat. "How did you know I was wearing a Stetson? You could tell I was a man with good taste?"

Whitney didn't know one cowboy hat from another. The only thing she knew was that this one was gray felt, broad-brimmed, and shaped low over his forehead. And he looked devilishly handsome in it.

"I didn't know that. I just thought that's what most Texas men wore."

"Hey, now, let's not get me confused with a Texas man," he said quickly.

"You live almost on the border," she defended her comment. "Surely there's not much difference."

He cast her a dry look. "I'll forgive you for your ignorance, Whitney. But only because you're a Yankee and because you look so damn pretty today."

Color spread across her cheeks. "Well, I suppose that makes up for being ignorant—in some cases," she said, making Caleb laugh again.

Whitney hadn't known what to wear this morning. Caleb hadn't said where they would be going or what they'd be doing. To play it safe, she'd dressed in navy-blue linen slacks and a matching blouse with red braiding setting off the square collar. She'd tied her hair back with a red bow and dabbed red lipstick on her lips. Whitney hadn't really taken pains with her appearance, but Caleb seemed to think so, and the idea made her feel warm and feminine.

A few minutes later Caleb slowed the pickup and turned off the highway. Whitney looked around her, seeing they had stopped in front of a long metal building painted a sickly yellow color. Junk cars were parked all around it and out in front near the highway sat a yellow wrecker with the word "Spider" written across the door.

"This is where my Jaguar is!" Whitney gasped. The place was little more than a dump and out in the middle of nowhere. There wasn't anything else to be seen except the empty highway and pine woods.

"That's right," Caleb said with a smugness that made Whitney want to cradle her forehead with both hands. "Now, come on, let's go see Spider and see how things are coming along."

Whitney couldn't believe that Caleb expected her to get out of the pickup. "You expect me to go in there? There's grease all over the ground and—"

Caleb shrugged. "I could carry you. But it wouldn't help your matter with Spider. He already thinks you're a crazy woman for backing into that pine tree."

Whitney suddenly bristled. "Oh, he does? Well, for his information, I didn't back into it. I slid into it!"

"Then maybe you'd better get out and tell him so."

Whitney licked her lips, then reached for the door handle. "I will. I'll also tell him how outrageous I think it is for taking two weeks to repair my car!"

Caleb smiled to himself as he climbed down from the truck and watched Whitney tiptoe around the hood to meet him.

"It won't come off on your shoes," he told her, speaking of the oil that had soaked into the red soil around the garage. "Spider pours it out here to keep down the dust."

Whitney wasn't sure she believed him, but she put her heels down anyway. They walked over to the building and Caleb pushed open the door.

The inside of the garage looked no better than the outside. Four vehicles were parked at odd angles to each other. Two had their hoods thrown up, a pickup was jacked off all four wheels and another had a crunched-in fender. Her white Jaguar was nowhere in sight.

"Spider? Are you under there somewhere?" Caleb called out.

Whitney stood close to Caleb's side while she looked around the chaotic garage. Greasy rags, tools and other mechanical-looking gadgets were tossed and piled at random. Whitney couldn't imagine anyone putting their car into Spider's hands. Not willingly, that is.

There was a scraping noise on the concrete floor. Whitney turned her head to see a little man wearing striped coveralls and a polka-dotted welding cap roll out from beneath the elevated pickup.

"Hey, there, Caleb," he called in a friendly voice. "What are you up to, boy?"

The man stood, adjusted the cap and grinned a toothy grin at the two of them.

"How you doing, Spider?" Caleb greeted. "I've brought Miss Drake. She's the lady from New York with the Jaguar."

The little man pulled a rag from his hip pocket, wiped his hand, then thrust it at Whitney.

"Nice to meet you, Miss Drake," he said, grinning and holding her hand with pointed pleasure. "That's a fine machine you have there. Real classy. We don't see too many of them in this part of the woods.''

Whitney couldn't help but smile back at Spider. The man couldn't be all bad, she thought. He obviously knew fine workmanship when he saw it.

"Thank you, Spider. Although I'm afraid it's not too classy now."

He patted her arm in a reassuring way. "But it will be. I'll have that little car of yours shinin' like a new penny. No one will ever know you backed into that tree."

"But I didn't—" Whitney began, only to have Spider cut her off.

"Just come on back here and I'll show you what I've done to her so far."

Spider took off through the narrow maze of black greasy junk iron. Whitney looked helplessly up at Caleb. But all he did was smile and motion with his head for her to follow.

The Jaguar was sitting outside behind the building beneath a scraggy elm tree. A tarp was thrown over a big part of it. Whitney wanted to weep at the sight of the car she'd once been so proud of.

Purchasing the car had been a goal in her life, a symbol of her success in the advertising industry. Now sitting here in a junky backyard, broken down and crunched in, it didn't seem like a symbol of anything except her own foolishness.

Spider pulled off the tarp and Whitney stared at the trunk of the car. Most of the wrinkles had been beaten out. In places the white paint had been sanded down to the shiny metal.

"I've still got quite a bit of work to go on her," Spider said. "I've been pretty swamped this past week. Ol' Grady, the mail carrier, his pickup broke down and everybody was a puttin' up a fuss for their mail. I'll be danged if it didn't take me a whole day to get him back on the road. But we'll get her, Miss Drake," he assured her.

"What about the driveline?" Caleb asked. "Has it been shipped to you, yet?"

Spider pushed back his cap and scratched the spiky black hair beneath it. "Naw, it hasn't. We're still not sure if it's gonna come from Dallas or New Orleans. But once we locate one, it'll be here in a day or two."

Caleb glanced down to see the bemused look on Whitney's face. "So when do you think you'll have the car finished completely?" he directed at the mechanic.

Spider scratched his head again. "Oh, I'd say about another week and a half. Give or take a day or two."

"How does that sound to you, Whitney?" Caleb asked.

It sounded like a long time to her. She'd only been with Caleb a small amount of time, but already she felt very drawn to him. How would she feel after a week and a half?

"It sounds fine," she finally blurted out. It was obvious Spider was doing the best he could, and she didn't want to be difficult about things. Wouldn't her father and friends laugh about that? she thought. Back in New York she was difficult about anything that slowed down her pace.

"Good," Caleb said. "Then we'd better be going and let Spider get back to work."

The three of them started back into the garage. Along the way Spider questioned Whitney about New York City.

"I've always wanted to see the Empire State Building," he said wistfully. "And one of those subway trains. Do you ever ride the subway, Miss Drake?"

Whitney shook her head. "If I need to go very far I drive or take a taxi."

Her answer seemed to disappoint him. He said, "Well, I sure would like to ride one and see how it works."

"Spider," Caleb spoke up, "you'd get up there in the city and a street gang would make a hood ornament out of you."

They were back in the garage now. Before Whitney knew what was happening, Spider jerked himself into a karate-type stance, his arms raised at Caleb.

"Hood ornament," he snorted. "Caleb, you know these hands of mine are lethal weapons. You ain't a-wearin' your gun today. Try me, just try me."

Wide-eyed, Whitney looked on. She didn't know whether to laugh, or throw herself bodily between the two men.

Caleb held up his hands in a surrendering gesture. "Spider, don't hurt me and make me look helpless in front of Miss Whitney. I've been trying all week to impress her."

Spider cackled loudly, obviously enjoying himself. "Go on, sport. I'll let you off today."

As she and Caleb climbed back into his pickup she asked, "Are you sure that man knows what he's doing?"

This raised a laugh from Caleb that had Whitney pursing her lips.

"I assure you there's no one that would do a better job. Why do you ask?"

Why did she ask! "Well, because he seems so..." She didn't know how to finish without sounding snobbish.

"Homespun?" he finished for her.

"Yes, something like that," Whitney agreed.

"Well, Spider is homespun. But that's the way he likes himself. The only time he was ever out of Louisiana was when he was in the army and served in Vietnam. That's where he learned how to be a mechanic."

"Oh, I see," she said, feeling suddenly ashamed of herself.

"Do you?" he asked, glancing at her. "I hope you do. Because Spider might be lacking refinement, but he's brimming over with heart. He has seven children. Three of the oldest he's put through college. He's very proud of that achievement. He takes pride in his work, too. He won't give you a slipshod job on the car."

Whitney looked over to meet his gaze. "You think I'm a snob, don't you?" she asked in a faintly accusing tone.

Caleb shook his head. "No, Whitney. I think you're just not used to people like Spider. Or even people like me," he added, a little grin curling up one corner of his mouth.

He was definitely right about that. She couldn't imagine finding anyone like Caleb if she looked all over the world.

"And I imagine if you took me to the city, your friends might call me redneck," he went on. "But that wouldn't offend me. The world is too big and wonderful to worry about a trivial little thing like social classes."

Whitney instinctively knew that Caleb was a man who could adapt to any situation or any crowd. It was she who had turned inside herself, away from those around her.

"I don't have that many friends anymore," she suddenly blurted her thoughts.

"I don't believe that for a minute," he said.

Whitney crossed her legs and turned in the seat so that she was facing him. "Well, it's true. I never was much of a socializer, although the few friends I did have I considered close. These past months though, everyone seemed to be excluding me from their lives."

Caleb frowned in contemplation. "That must have hurt."

A stark look settled over Whitney's features. "I told myself I didn't give a damn. I didn't need them anyway."

"So you lied to yourself instead of facing the problem."

Whitney gasped softly. "I didn't lie to myself! If they don't need me, I don't need them."

Caleb drummed his fingers against the steering wheel. Whitney forced her eyes back on the scenery. They were obviously getting closer to a town. Houses were beginning to appear on either side of the highway. Many of them were brick with huge, beautifully landscaped yards.

"What happened? You develop a contagious disease?"

Whitney laughed shakily and some of the tension drained out of her. "Funny you should use those words. My dearest friend accused me of being a workaholic. She said there was no use in calling me anymore because I didn't have time to be her friend."

"Well, was she right?" Caleb asked.

"I used to think not," Whitney said, her head dropping. "But now, I don't know anymore, Caleb. Now that I've gotten away from everything I can see that maybe I was on the wrong track." She shrugged and looked up at him. "But even so, the damage is already done. Admitting something isn't going to change it all back."

"No," Caleb said thoughtfully. "But it will make things better for you in the future."

Whitney didn't say anything. She was busy thinking back to a few days ago. She hadn't even thought of herself as having a future. But Caleb had changed that with his smile, his laughter, his positive outlook. He was making her think she could actually believe in herself again.

Whitney fell in love with Natchitoches as Caleb leisurely drove her through the quiet, narrow streets, point-

ing out many old gracious Southern homes that had been
built years before the turn of the century. The river running through the city was also enchanting, although Caleb
only allowed her a brief look. He wanted her to see it at
night, he told her, because he was a true romantic.

Caleb took her to lunch in a small, out of the way café
where the waitress and even the cook knew him on a first-
name basis. They ate a dish called Dirty Rice and Beans.
Caleb tried to get her to try the boiled crawdads and fried
frog legs, but Whitney told him she needed to inch into
Cajun cooking instead of jumping in all at once.

Once the meal was over they headed out of town on
Highway 1. The highway eventually led to Alexandria, but
today Caleb took it to show Whitney the plantations that
could be seen a few miles out of Natchitoches.

Whitney marveled at the preserved history in the grace-
ful old mansions with their yards shaded with huge oaks
and cypress trees. Behind many of the houses were an-
cient groves of pecan trees that, Caleb informed her, had
once supported the plantations.

It was growing dusky dark by the time they headed back
to Natchitoches. Before they reached the city, Caleb pulled
over at a small country store and parked the truck.

"Why are you stopping here?" Whitney asked, looking
at the small store with its wooden screen door and windows plastered with assorted signs and posters.

"To buy your supper," Caleb informed her. He came
around and opened the door.

Reaching for his hand, Whitney climbed from the truck.
"This doesn't look like an eating place," she said, taking
another look at the building.

There was a set of gas pumps in front. Presently a man
was filling his pickup truck. Three children were sitting in
the back, along with a fuzzy red dog. The long ends of

cane fishing poles stuck out over the tailgate. The two young boys were wrestling playfully while the older girl sat quietly staring at Whitney. There was a look on her face that reminded Whitney of the homeless on the city streets.

It was a wistful, hungry look, a look that reminded Whitney how fortunate she really was. Not just because she had financial security, but because someone like Caleb cared about her. And he did care about her, she thought. Maybe just as a friend, but he did care, and that made her feel good and warm inside.

"Why there's Mr. Jones," a large woman greeted as they stepped inside the store. She was standing behind a long wooden counter and she smiled with pleasure at the sight of Caleb.

"Hello, Beulah. How's my favorite girlfriend?" Caleb asked.

Beulah rolled her eyes toward the back of the store. "Don't you let Henry hear you!" she hissed. "You know how jealous he is! And a good-looking thing like you coming in here and sweet-talking me. Why, you're just asking for murder!"

Caleb laughed under his breath. "Beulah, if you weren't so much of a woman, Henry wouldn't be so jealous."

Beulah grinned sassily at Caleb, then glanced at Whitney. "You got a new girlfriend?"

"This is Miss Whitney Drake. She's from New York City," Caleb introduced, then gave the woman an exasperated look. "But Beulah, I thought *you* were my girlfriend."

Beulah nodded a hello to Whitney, then darted her eyes anxiously toward the back of the store. "Henry is going to be back any minute now, Caleb. So you just hush that kind of talk!"

Still laughing, Caleb said, "Okay, Beulah. I'll hush if you'll fix Whitney and me one of your bologna sandwiches."

"Now that I will do," Beulah said, walking over to an ancient-looking meat box. "You want the works on 'em?"

"The works," Caleb agreed.

While the woman made the sandwiches, Caleb pulled a soft drink out of an old cooler and invited Whitney to choose what she'd like to drink.

She chose a cola, then sipped it slowly as she wandered through the store's small aisles. Caleb strolled along beside her, pointing out the things he liked and disliked to eat and asking Whitney her preferences.

There were no other customers in the store. It was quiet except for a radio playing near the checkout counter. Beulah had just finished making the sandwiches when a thin man came through a door at the back of the room. A broad smile spread over his face when he spotted Caleb.

"Hello, Henry. How's it going?" Caleb asked.

"Fine, Mr. Jones. Just fine. Where's your badge and gun today? You taking a day off?"

With a crooked grin and a possessive glint in his eye, Caleb wound his arm around Whitney's waist. "When a beautiful woman like Whitney is around, I can't concentrate on work. You know the feeling, Henry."

Henry laughed. "That's what I've been telling my Beulah for years. She's just so pretty all I want to do is sit all day long and look at her."

From behind the meat counter Beulah snorted loudly. "Henry, you quit that lying! Caleb knows why you want to sit all day. You're lazy! It's plain and simple. Ain't got nothing to do with the way I look!"

Henry winked at Caleb and Whitney.

Caleb spoke up. "Beulah, don't be jumping on Henry. He can't help it because he's so taken by your beauty."

Beulah came out from behind the counter carrying two packages wrapped in waxed paper.

"Caleb, I was going to give you a pickle to go with your sandwich, but now I'm just going to give your girlfriend one, 'cause you're as ornery as Henry!"

She handed them their supper. Whitney thanked her while Caleb said, "Henry, is your wife always this mean?"

"Mean as a snake," Henry agreed. "That's why I sleep with one eye open."

Beulah plopped her hands on her hips and gave her husband a hard look, making Caleb laugh and Whitney smile. It was obvious the couple were crazy about each other.

"Before you two go at each other, I want Henry to get me a bag of his shelled pecans. Pearl will bake a pecan pie if I get them for her."

"How is Miss Pearl?" Beulah asked as Henry left to get the pecans.

"Pearl is as sassy as ever," Caleb answered.

The three of them began to walk back to the checkout counter. Whitney was acutely aware when Caleb dropped his arm from her waist. The warm imprint of his touch stayed with her as he took out his billfold and counted out the money for their purchases.

"I haven't seen her in a long time," Beulah said. "You need to bring her over more often, Caleb."

"Pearl's not much of a goer. I have to work hard to get her off the place. But I'll tell her you'd like a visit," he promised.

Henry appeared with the pecans, and after exchanged farewells, Whitney and Caleb walked back to the truck.

Once they were traveling down the highway again, Whitney asked, "Is everyone in this area always so friendly?"

"Most everyone," he answered.

"And they all know you," she said. "You must either have a reputation, or cover a lot of territory."

Caleb grinned. "Both, I suppose."

She cut him a suspicious glance beneath her dark lashes. "And I suppose your reputation is for being a rascal?"

He feigned a hurt look. "Whitney, do I look like a rascal?"

He looked like a strong, virile man on the outside, but on the inside she suspected he was very soft and gentle.

Whitney smiled to herself as she sipped the remainder of her cola. "I think I agree with Beulah. You're ornery."

"Ornery! Do you mean ornery, like lazy? Or ornery like irritating?"

"Irritating fits you perfectly."

"Well, I'm hurt now, Whitney. Really hurt."

There was such a wounded sound to his voice that Whitney looked over at him surprise.

"Caleb, I was only teasing!"

With a shocked expression Caleb reached over and placed his hand against her brow. "My God, is she sick? Or is she actually having fun?"

Grimacing, Whitney swatted his hand away, but then she began to laugh. "You are irritating!"

"But I made you laugh," he countered.

Whitney's eyes were soft as she smiled over at him. "Yes, you did."

For seconds they merely looked at each other, then Caleb was forced to put his eyes back on the highway.

At that moment Whitney realized she had become closer to Caleb than anyone else in her life for a long, long time.

It was a good thing to be beside him, to talk with him, to laugh with him. But the whole thing frightened her, too.

She wasn't the type of woman who would interest a man like Caleb for very long. She wasn't a woman whom any man would care deeply about. Edward and her father had proved that to her.

Chapter Nine

"What are you thinking, Whitney? You've lost your smile."

A small sigh escaped her as she looked over at him. "I was thinking that I like your Louisiana, Caleb. Just like you promised."

"Does that mean you've forgotten about Padre Island?"

Padre Island? So much had happened since the night of her accident that she had to stop and remember that that was where she had been heading in the first place.

"I suppose so. After all, you said there wasn't anything there but beaches and oily bodies."

Caleb laughed. "I just said that to soothe you, Whitney. It's a nice place to visit."

Her brows lifted. "Have you really been there, or were you just saying that, too?"

He shook his head. "Yes, I've really been there. Although it's been several years ago. Would you like to go anyway? I have several days of leave coming to me, we could make a time of it."

At first it shocked Whitney that he would take time off from his job to vacation with her. It was a flattering and an even more appealing thought. But it was also a scary one. Thrown together in such a romantic situation, she would surely lose her heart to him. Whereas, she was certain Caleb would view the whole thing as just fun in the sun.

"I think I'd rather just stay here in Louisiana," she said, her gaze dropping. "I'm beginning to love the tall pine trees and the beautiful azaleas and wisterias. And believe it or not, the quiet."

"What about the people?" Caleb asked.

Whitney thought she detected a serious note in his voice, but she couldn't be sure. "The people are very nice, too. Including you. You're not really all that ornery," she ended on a teasing note.

"I'm glad to hear that," he said with a smile. He was disappointed that she'd turned down the offer to go to Padre Island with him, but he wasn't going to push the issue. She was beginning to show him there was a sweet, easy side to her. He didn't want to risk ruining the fragile relationship they'd built together.

"Do you want to eat the sandwiches now, or do you want to wait until we're on the boat?"

"The boat?"

They were approaching the city of Natchitoches. Whitney could see the lights up ahead of them.

"Yes. Remember I was going to show you the river tonight?"

"I remember. But I didn't know we were going by boat. I didn't know you owned a boat," she told him.

"I don't. But I have a friend who does. He lets me use it whenever I like."

"Generous friend," she mused aloud, while wondering if she could trust herself to be alone with Caleb in a boat under the moonlight.

"I've done a few favors for him," Caleb commented. "But good friends don't measure things like that."

Whitney looked at him in the darkness, but said nothing. She didn't want to think about the friends who'd distanced themselves from her. She only wanted to think about Caleb and the positive difference he'd made in her life.

Once they were in town Caleb wound through the residential area until he located a modest white house shaded by a massive magnolia tree. There was no car in the driveway when Caleb pulled in and shut off the motor.

"It looks like no one is home," Caleb said, surveying the dark house.

"Well, perhaps we can do it another time," Whitney suggested, not sure if she was disappointed or relieved about missing the boat trip.

Grabbing the sandwiches, Caleb reached for the door handle. "Just because Phil isn't home doesn't mean we can't use the boat. I know where he keeps the key."

He climbed out of the truck and came around to help Whitney down to the ground.

"But isn't that rather presumptuous of you? Just to take the man's boat? Maybe we'd better wait," she said in a guarded voice.

Caleb laughed. "Whitney, darlin', I thought you were getting over all that fretting and nervousness. Now come along," he invited, curling his arm around her slender waist. "I promise Phil won't have us clapped in irons for borrowing his boat. Besides, I'm the law, remember?"

How could Whitney forget? Everywhere they went people referred to him as an authority figure. In the past
Whitney had been the authority figure in her workplace.
As a boss she could easily deal with people. But as a friend,
a daughter and fiancée, she had failed abysmally. It was a
sobering reminder not to open her heart to anyone.

Caleb guided her behind the house and across a small
lawn enclosed in a chainlink fence. They passed through a
gate and headed down a sloping embankment that Whitney could see led to the river.

"Watch your step," Caleb warned as the ground grew
even steeper.

Whitney gripped his hand until they reached a small
boat house built over the river's edge. Inside Caleb flipped
a light switch. Floating between two wooden walkways was
a blue and silver craft with a divided windshield and cush-
ioned seats on the bow. Whitney gave a small gasp of
pleasure at the sight.

"This is very nice," she told Caleb.

"Yes. I've been thinking for a long time about getting
one of my own. But then I decided I wouldn't use it that
much."

"Because of your job? Caleb," she scolded lightly,
"you're the person who's been preaching fun and relaxation to me."

He laughed a little sheepishly as he took her arm to help
her into the boat.

"I know, Whitney. But I don't have anyone at home to
share my time with. If I did, I wouldn't work as much. I
probably would buy a boat like this, take vacations and
play in the sun and the water."

Did he mean a wife? Whitney wondered. He was bachelor material, but for some reason it was easy for her to see
Caleb with a wife, even with children. She instinctively

knew that once he committed himself to one woman he
would be true to her for life. He was a man of integrity. He
was also a man with a capacity for love, deep and strong.

"I can see you on a beach, Caleb, with a child riding on
each shoulder."

He grinned broadly as he stepped into the boat to join
her. "Nice thought, isn't it. I've always wanted children.
What about you?"

She'd never really had a deep longing for children before. Edward hadn't inspired that kind of loving or shar-
ing in her. But now as she looked at Caleb she was getting
all kinds of maternal feelings. It was a jolting realization.

"I— Children would be nice," she said in a hushed
voice. "With the right man."

Beneath the dim light Caleb's eyes roamed over Whitney's face. There was a soft, wistful look on her features.
He felt himself reaching out for her in spite of the caution
running through his head.

"Am I that man, Whitney?"

His fingers were entwined with hers, his other hand on
her face. As Whitney looked up at him she had the great-
est urge to step into his arms, to tell him that she wanted
nothing more than to give herself to him.

But she couldn't do that, she desperately argued with
herself. She barely knew this man. And even if she did, he
probably didn't want her the way she wanted him. As
someone to love, now and forever.

Someone to love! The words rocketed through her brain.
Was she falling in love with Caleb? God, it couldn't be, she
thought desperately. She wasn't ready to open herself up
to that kind of pain.

Caleb watched as a dark, panicky look filled her brown
eyes, and knew his question had backed her into a corner.

It was a moment before she could collect herself enough to speak. When she did, she forced her words and voice to be teasing. "Caleb, just think of all your little old ladies. It would break their hearts if you ever married."

"They'd eventually get over it," he assured her. His voice was husky, his eyelids lowered sensually down at Whitney.

Her heart began to bang away. "I doubt it," she murmured a bit breathlessly as his head began to inch down toward hers.

Caleb's lips tasted hers gently, as though to give her the chance to back away if she wanted to. But Whitney couldn't back away. Each time Caleb kissed her it pulled at something deep inside her, something that made her want to reach out and hold on to him. Not just for the moment, but for always. It was such a profound feeling that it left her shaking.

"Caleb, the boat is swaying," she whispered once he'd lifted his lips from hers.

"That's not the boat, Whitney. That's my heart tilting," he said. He pulled her hand up flat against his chest. "See what you do to me, darlin'?"

His heart was indeed beating fast and hard. To think that she might have actually affected him that much brought a warm color to her cheeks and for a moment she forgot the racing of her own heart.

She dropped her eyes from his. Her voice was a bit breathy as she said, "Caleb, half the time I never know if you're serious or teasing."

Over her head he drew in a deep breath. "Why don't we take our boat ride, and while we're out on the water maybe you can figure that out."

Whitney was so shaken she doubted she could think one coherent thought, but she nodded at him anyway and let him help her onto a padded seat. She was silent as Caleb got behind the driver's wheel and started the motor.

Inside the small boat house, the engine's noise was deafening, but once Caleb backed the boat out into the river, the sound didn't seem too loud anymore.

He put the boat into gear and they began to glide forward at a leisurely pace. "Here," he said, handing her one of the wrapped sandwiches. "Let's have our supper."

Whitney was glad to have something to focus her attention on. She unwrapped the sandwich and took a bite.

Caleb said, "Beulah has the best bologna I've ever eaten. I guess it's rather late to be asking if you like bologna."

"Rather late," she agreed in a dry voice, then looked at him pointedly in the dark. "I'd like to know where you get the idea that I'm going to like all the things you like? Does being a lawman do that to you?"

Her question had him laughing and the sound carried across the still water around them. "Why, Whitney, I just think you'll like them because I only like good things."

Whitney frowned. "That doesn't quite make sense, Caleb. But there is one thing I know. I'd love to get you in New York City for a few days."

He grinned over at her as he bit into his sandwich. "Would you entertain me? If you say yes, we'll go tomorrow."

"I was thinking more in the line of turning you loose in a deli," she said, trying to ignore that this was the second time he'd insinuated he wanted to spend more time with her.

He chuckled and then he grew serious as he looked ahead and steered the boat. "I'd like for us to go up to the top of the Statue of Liberty together. I'd like to put my arm around your shoulders and look out over the harbor and think about all the people who'd come to this country and eventually given their lives to make it free and wonderful for us." He looked over at her and smiled rather whimsically. "Sounds corny, doesn't it? But I don't care. I like the idea anyway."

Surprisingly Whitney felt a sting of moisture in her eyes. Such a simple thing, she thought, to look out over a harbor with a man. But when that man was Caleb the whole idea took on a different meaning. Maybe, she thought warily, maybe he had been serious minutes ago when they'd talked of children.

"I—I think it's a very nice idea," she said in a low voice. She looked down at her half-eaten sandwich and realized she was gripping it.

She didn't sound as if she meant it was a nice idea, Caleb thought. But then she'd just come from New York, and she'd obviously left problems behind her there. Knowing that should have been enough to put him off Whitney, but no matter what Caleb told himself, he felt himself drawn to her anyway.

"What do you think about the river?" he asked after a moment.

Whitney looked around her. The river was not wide enough for large, commercial use. It was more the size of a two-lane highway with steep grassy embankments on either side. Above them were residential and commercial establishments. Lights twinkled from many of them, shining down like stars on the water, just as Caleb had promised.

"I think it's very beautiful," she said truthfully. It was strange how meeting and getting to know Caleb had made her so much more aware of the nature around her. He'd opened her eyes to so many things that had gone unnoticed before in her life.

They continued to travel upriver, each of them in thoughtful silence as they finished their sandwiches. Along the way they passed several boats of odd shapes and sizes.

After a few moments Caleb said, "Come over here by me. You can drive the boat for a while."

Whitney eyed the narrow scat behind the steering wheel. She'd have to practically sit in his lap. "I've never driven a boat before," she hedged.

"Nothing to it," he assured her. "Come here and I'll show you."

"I'd better not. Remember, I've already crashed my Jaguar," she said, hoping he would think she was afraid of wrecking the boat instead of being close to him.

He laughed softly, then reached across and curled his hand around hers. With a gentle tug he pulled her across the small space separating the seats.

"Caleb! I don't want to do this!"

He made room for her, keeping his arm curled snugly around her shoulders as she sat next to him.

"Sure you do," he said with a know-it-all drawl that had Whitney compressing her lips and looking directly into his face.

"There you go again! Taking me for granted, thinking I'm going to like this, just because you do. For your information I— Caleb!"

While she'd been talking, he'd let go of the steering wheel. The boat was veering off to the left, heading on a straight course toward the bank.

"Caleb, do something!" she cried.

"You're the driver now. You do something," he told her calmly.

They were only a few feet away from the bank and it was obvious he wasn't going to lift a finger to steer the boat. Whitney grabbed the steering wheel and turned it to the right. Much to her relief, the craft instantly began to straighten its course.

"See, it's just like driving a car. Nothing to it. All you have to do is watch the traffic and don't make any abrupt turns."

Whitney tentatively turned the steering wheel, getting the feel of it beneath her hands. After a moment she smiled up at Caleb.

"You're right, it is easy. How do you do the gears and the gas?"

To his far right was a throttle that moved backward and forward. Caleb pulled it to the middle.

"This is neutral. Otherwise forward is forward and backward is reverse. The more you push, the more gas you give it."

Whitney nodded that she understood and placed her hand firmly on the throttle.

"There's a button on top of the handle that locks the gear shift," Caleb told her. "Push it down to release it, then you can go forward slowly," he added.

"Yes, slowly," she repeated, doing as he instructed.

The boat began to move forward once again and Whitney looked proudly up at him. "How was that?"

One side of his golden-brown mustache lifted as he grinned down at her. "You're a natural, Whitney."

Whitney felt her breath catch in her throat. He was so good to look at, and she was all too aware that her back and shoulder were pressed against his chest.

"Thank you, Caleb," she said.

"For what?" he asked, his eyes drifting over her black hair. It and her skin smelled of jasmine, and he wondered if the scent was making him a little drunk, or maybe it was the feel of her against him, all soft and warm and womanly.

"For showing me the river tonight. For the bologna sandwich, for the whole day," she added on a soft sigh. "I've enjoyed it."

He smiled over her head. "Well, shucks, Whitney, it was nothing," he drawled with exaggerated modesty. "I had a hard time trying to decide between a French restaurant and the opera, or the river and bologna. I'm glad I made the right choice."

She laughed at that and Caleb's hand tightened on her shoulder, making Whitney tilt her head back and up to see his face.

Caleb couldn't think about caution or doubt as his eyes drank in the beauty of her face now bathed in moonlight. He leaned down to take her lips.

Whitney closed her eyes, thinking she could go on kissing Caleb and never grow tired. She could always be near him and never feel the need to move away. Unconsciously her hand slipped from the steering wheel to slide up and around his neck. Caleb tightened his hold on her, deepening the kiss, drawing on her lips with a fervor that robbed Whitney of her breath.

The kiss lasted much longer than either of them realized and would have gone on if the boat hadn't rammed into the bank. The jolt knocked them apart, leaving Whitney dazed and gasping, and Caleb cursing softly under his breath.

Quickly he grabbed the throttle and put the boat in reverse. Her face flaming with embarrassment, Whitney scooted over to the passenger's seat.

"Is...the boat harmed?" she asked as Caleb maneuvered the craft back on its proper course.

Caleb shook his head. "I don't think so. We weren't traveling fast enough."

"I guess my driving didn't prove so great after all," she said in a small voice.

Caleb glanced over at her as he caught the dismal note in her voice. He'd known before that she was a sensitive person, but he realized it even more now.

Reaching out and softly touching her cheek, he said, "Good, Lord, Whitney, I'm glad you were thinking about me instead of driving the boat. Because I certainly had my mind on you."

Yes, she believed he had been thinking of her, and she was suddenly aware that their relationship was moving at a speed that was threatening to get out of control.

Whitney knew she couldn't let that happen. She'd always been in control of things before, and she had to stay in control of her feelings now, before she wound up a loser again.

"Well," she said, drawing a deep breath. "I'm glad the boat isn't damaged."

She dragged a hand through her hair, then reached for her purse and drew out a cigarette.

Caleb watched her fumble with the lighter and knew she was upset. He wondered if it was because of the kiss they'd shared, or because the boat had run aground. He wanted to think it was because of the kiss, he wanted to think she was beginning to care for him. Because he couldn't deny, even to himself, that he was beginning to care for her.

As soon as Whitney opened her eyes the next morning, she knew she had slept late. Throwing on her robe, she went out to the kitchen to discover that Caleb had already left for work.

There was a note attached with a piece of cellophane tape to the refrigerator door.

Whitney,
You were sleeping so peacefully, I hated to wake you.
See you tonight.

Caleb.

The note made her smile, just as Caleb made her smile. Then she realized she was already thinking ahead to tonight, looking forward to Caleb coming home.

Oh, Whitney, she groaned to herself. What have you done? Run from one giant mistake, straight into the arms of another one? she asked herself.

But how could caring for Caleb be so wrong, she wondered, when everything about it felt so right? He wasn't like her father, he wasn't like Edward. But she was that same woman who hadn't lived up to either man's standards, she reminded herself. What made her think it would be any different with Caleb?

He was a man who obviously didn't have trouble attracting women. The fact that he was near thirty and still not married proved he must be particular where women were concerned. Even though Caleb was a man who teased and enjoyed himself, he was also a man who had deep values and high standards. Could she prove herself worthy of his love?

The question made her realize just how far her feelings for Caleb had come. Sometime, from the moment she'd first met him up until now, love had sparked in her heart, begging her to reach out to him.

It was a scary thought to Whitney, one that almost made her want to get back out on the highway and start running again. Almost, but not quite. Something told her that Caleb could be the most important thing that ever happened to her.

Last night she'd told herself to get her feelings under control, but now she knew it was too late for that. It was also too late for running. Her heart was already on the line, out in the open. She just wondered what Caleb intended to do with it.

Chapter Ten

Whitney dressed in a pair of sand-colored slacks and a sleeveless sweater of matching cotton knit. She ate a light breakfast then went about making the beds, washing the dishes and picking up odds and ends lying around the house.

The finished tasks gave her a contented feeling, and she looked around the rooms of the old house, wondering if Caleb would notice the work she'd done and be surprised by it.

Just before noon she walked over to Pearl's house. The old woman's voice called out when Whitney knocked on the door. She followed the sound of it through the house and out onto a screened-in back porch. Pearl was up to her elbows in potting soil and an overgrown philodendron.

"Hello, Whitney. How are you this morning?"

"Very well, Pearl. And you?"

"I wished I'd never started this job," she snorted. "But it was either that or throw the thing away."

"That would have been a crime," Whitney said, fingering a leaf of the healthy green plant.

Pearl began to tamp the dark soil around the roots. Without looking up at Whitney, she said, "I suppose you and Caleb had a good time yesterday. You were out all day."

Whitney noticed the old woman stated the words as if she knew without asking. The idea made Whitney's mouth curve into a faint smile.

"Yes, we did," Whitney replied. "Caleb showed me around the area. And we also checked on my car."

"And what did Spider have to say about it?" Pearl asked.

Whitney continued to examine the leaf between her fingers. "A week or more, depending on a few things."

"That's good," Pearl said. "You haven't been around here near long enough."

Whitney looked up curiously. "Why do you say that?"

Pearl continued with her work. "You're still skinny and pale and still worn-out lookin'."

Whitney frowned. "I didn't know I looked that terrible."

Pearl shook her head, then glanced up at Whitney. "You're a beautiful young woman. You just look like you need a bit of a change."

Whitney sighed and moved away from Pearl's worktable to take a seat in a lawn chair. "I suppose I did need a change, Pearl. I'd been having lots of rows with my father. You see, we worked together at his advertising firm. But then he fired me and—well, I was pretty upset about it. I guess it all took a toll on me."

"I should say so," Pearl said with concern. "What did you do that was so all-fired bad that your daddy had to fire you?"

Whitney still felt pangs of hurt when she thought of that final day she'd argued with her father. He'd said in the end that she would thank him for firing her. However, Whitney still couldn't fully fathom his actions.

Her eyes fell from Pearl's. "Not any one particular thing, Pearl. He said it had become impossible to work with me. You see, with Father, his business is everything. It's even more important than family."

Pearl made a tsking noise with her tongue. "Can't say I agree with the man. What's stronger than family blood? Besides, everyone goes off track now and then. Maybe you just needed nudging back on track."

Whitney let out a wistful sigh. She hadn't meant to get into all this. It brought back depressing memories, and the day was too beautiful for her to be depressed.

"I met a friend of yours yesterday," Whitney said brightly, changing the subject completely. "She wants you to come for a visit."

"Oh? Who was it?"

"A woman named Beulah. She runs a general store."

Pearl smiled with fondness. "Yes. I do need to see Beulah. I made a pair of throw pillows for her in exchange for some of Henry's pecans. I never have gotten them to her yet."

Whitney smiled to herself, remembering the pecans Caleb had purchased for Pearl. He'd probably surprise her with them tonight.

"She fixed Caleb and me a bologna sandwich. It was very good."

Pearl, finished with the plant, reached to hang it on a hook on the wall. "Beulah and Henry are fine, hard-working people. They lost their only son about a year ago in a car wreck. He was their joy, the only child they were able to have."

Whitney felt terribly sad as she thought of the couple. "They seemed so happy," she murmured thoughtfully.

"That's because they are happy, Whitney. Even though they lost their son, they know they're still blessed in other ways. And they have each other."

The old woman said the last words as though having a mate to love was the most important thing in the world. Whitney had never thought so before, but now that she'd met Caleb, she was beginning to believe it was true.

Pearl wiped her hands on her apron, then reached down and patted Whitney on the knee. "Come along and we'll find something for lunch."

A few minutes later the two women were sitting at Pearl's kitchen table eating tuna sandwiches and drinking iced tea.

Both sets of Whitney's grandparents had passed on by the time she was still a small girl. So Whitney had never had much of an opportunity to be with older people. She was finding she enjoyed Pearl's company immensely. There was something very reassuring about the wisdom and stability of a person who'd lived as long as Pearl.

Whitney looked across at Pearl with fondness. "Do you think there's a chance I could possibly learn to cook?"

Pearl's thin brows lifted with curiosity. "You want to learn how to cook?"

"Is it difficult?"

Pearl chuckled as she reached for her glass. "Not really. You're bright. I'd say you'd catch on real fast. I'm just more curious as to why you're wanting to learn now, seeing you've gotten by twenty-eight years without knowing how."

Whitney felt color spread across her cheeks. "I've never needed to know before. Back in New York City I had a woman who did all the cooking. But now, well, I'd like to prepare something for Caleb. To surprise him with a meal tonight."

"Tonight! Girl, you can't learn to cook in one day. It takes a lot of practice."

Whitney felt sheepish. "Well, that's where you come in, Pearl. I thought you might come over and guide me through a meal."

Pearl leaned back in her chair, folded her arms across her breasts and smiled pointedly. "So this is the same woman who couldn't get away from this place fast enough?"

Whitney grimaced. "Pearl, that was days ago. I've had a chance to get used to things, and to know you and Caleb. I feel differently now."

"Hmm. Is that right?"

Whitney fidgeted with her teaspoon. "Yes, that's right. And I feel like I'd like to do something for Caleb. To let him know how much I appreciate his kindness."

Pearl smiled to herself. "Caleb is a kind man. Although I've never known his kindness to go this far."

Whitney looked up at the old woman. "What do you mean?"

Pearl took a long drink of her tea, then said, "Inviting you to stay in his home. I don't ever remember him doing such a thing before."

Whitney felt herself blushing once again. "That's probably because there hasn't been anyone else who had a wreck out here in the boondocks."

"Well, not anyone that looked like you," Pearl said with recollection. "Grover Johnson had a wreck out this way one time. But since he lives only about five miles away, Caleb just loaded him up and drove him home."

Whitney wondered dryly if Grover Johnson was any-thing like Spider, but before she could ask, Pearl was speaking again.

"Well, finish up your sandwich, Whitney, and we'll go over and check out Caleb's freezer. Surely we can find something you can cook for him tonight."

"Oh, you mean you'll help me?" Whitney asked with great relief.

Pearl leaned across the table and patted Whitney's hand. "'Course I'll help, and Caleb will never have to know."

Pearl informed Whitney that unless something out of the ordinary came up during the day, Caleb was usually home by six o'clock. At five-thirty the old woman left Caleb's kitchen to go back to her own house, and Whit-ney went to her bedroom to change her clothes.

The day had grown very hot so Whitney decided on a gathered pink skirt that struck her mid-calf, and a white blouse with a platter collar. She'd just finished winding her hair up into a simple twist when she heard his truck drive up. Her heart was beating with eager anticipation as she hurried out of the bedroom and walked onto the wooden porch.

Caleb was climbing from his truck, his pistol and hol-ster slung over his left shoulder.

Whitney walked slowly down the steps and out to meet him.

As she approached, he lifted his head and smiled broadly at the sight of her. Whitney couldn't help but smile back and reach for his hand once she was at his side.

Caleb leaned down and kissed her cheek. "I swear, Whitney, you're as pretty as a wildwood rose," he said.

Whitney had received compliments from men before, but none of them had ever touched her like this one. And suddenly seeing Caleb again had her feeling as if she were sixteen, her heart brimming with love, her whole life bright and beautiful before her.

"Thank you," she said, then squeezed his hand and gave him a sidelong glance. "I have a surprise for you."

Caleb darted her a curious glance. His thoughts had been on Whitney all day, of coming home to her. Now that he had, he realized that any chance of stopping his growing feelings for her was out of the question.

"Is it a good one, or a bad one?"

She smiled impishly and tugged him up the steps. "A good one, I think."

Inside the house, Caleb put his pistol away, then went to wash. While he did, Whitney hurried to the kitchen, to put the finishing touches on the meal. Earlier this afternoon she'd gone out in the yard and gathered several branches of azaleas. She'd put the red and white blossoms in a glass and placed them in the center of the table. Now she hurried over and began to dish the food onto their plates.

Caleb came into the room as she was placing the filled plates on the table. Surprised, he kept his eyes on Whitney as he took his seat.

"I thought you didn't know how to cook."

Whitney's lips curved into a tentative smile as she sat across from him. "Pearl gave me a few directions. But I did it all myself," she added proudly.

His eyes went back to his plate filled with a pork chop, fried okra, mashed potatoes and milk gravy. It was one of his favorite meals. "Whitney, you didn't have to do all this."

"I, well, I thought you might be tired and hungry. Anyway, yesterday was so lovely that I wanted to do something for you."

Caleb picked up his fork, but instead of eating he looked across the table at the eager light in Whitney's eyes. There was something about her that reminded him over and over that he was a man. He liked the feeling—far too much, he thought.

"Whitney," he said softly, "I didn't expect you to pay me back! Yesterday was something I wanted to do. Your company was all the payment I needed."

His words caused her heart to swell and her eyes met his blue ones. "That's very nice of you to say, Caleb," she said softly.

He shrugged and smiled, while inside he was fighting the urge to go around the table and pull her into his arms.

The evening was still hot and there was a damp sheen on her face and throat. The black fringe across her forehead had curled fiercely in the Louisiana humidity. Her beauty was inviting but not nearly as inviting as the look in her eyes.

"Well, I'm a nice guy—at times," he said teasingly.

She took a deep breath and looked down at her plate. "Well, we might as well try it," she suggested, nervously picking up her fork. "But please don't feel as if you have to eat it if it doesn't taste good," she added.

He chuckled under his breath and forked up a few pieces of the crisp okra. "I said I was nice, Whitney, not a glutton for punishment."

Whitney watched him intently, waiting anxiously for his reaction. Strange, she thought, but she'd never worried over or tried as hard on any ad campaign as she had this meal. Pleasing Caleb had become much more important to her than selling products for some faceless company.

"Well? How is it?"

Caleb swallowed the okra, fully aware that Whitney's dark brown eyes were glued to his face for the slightest reaction.

"Delicious."

The pent-up breath went out of her. "Really, Caleb? Are you sure?"

"Pearl couldn't have done better herself," he assured her.

She smiled a glorious smile at him, unaware that she had yet to take a bite from her own plate. "Try the mashed potatoes. Those were fun to do."

"Fun?" he asked wryly.

"Yes. I used the electric mixer on them and I'd never used one of those gadgets before," she explained.

Shaking his head, he laughed and tried the potatoes. They were surprisingly good. "Just right. Not too thin, not too stiff. Whitney, I think you took to cooking even better than you did to boat driving."

She felt color flood her cheeks. "Let's not talk about my boating skills. Besides, you were the instigator of that crash," she couldn't help adding.

Whitney was surprised to see a flush spread over Caleb's tanned face. Obviously he hadn't forgotten their kiss.

He shook his head. "No. It was all your fault, Whitney," he said.

"My fault?" she echoed in surprise.

He nodded as he picked up a knife and sliced into the chop. "That's right. If you hadn't looked so pretty I wouldn't have wanted to kiss you in the first place."

She slanted him a look from beneath her black lashes. "You know just when to be a charmer, don't you?"

"I'll take that as a compliment, Whitney," he said, then bit into a piece of chop with a beguiling grin.

After chewing and swallowing, he inclined his head toward Whitney's plate. "You haven't touched your food yet."

Whitney looked at the fork in her hand and realized she had been so caught up in Caleb that she'd forgotten all about eating herself.

It was unlike her to lose her head over anything, and she wondered why Caleb was bringing about this change in her. Did he have some magical, Southern touch that had cast a spell over her heart? It seemed so, for every moment she spent with him she felt herself falling more and more in love with him.

They ate in silence for a few moments. Then Caleb said, "The flowers are nice."

"I hope it didn't hurt the bushes to break them off," she told him.

Caleb shook his head. "Not at all. Azaleas thrive around here. I guess it's all the humidity."

Whitney's eyes fell on the white and crimson blossoms. If she wanted flowers back in New York, she called a florist. A delivery boy would bring them to the door and she'd pay him. It was convenient. But there had been something satisfying about gathering these flowers herself with the birds singing in the branches of the pines over her head, the sun sinking slowly behind the woods, and the thought of Caleb coming home.

Stop and smell the flowers, Caleb had told her. She was now beginning to see just what he'd meant.

"I don't suppose you have a place for flowers back in New York," he said. "But then I remember you saying you weren't a flower person anyway."

Whitney grimaced as she remembered telling him that flowers weren't worth the trouble since they only wilted.

God, she'd been in a horrible state of mind then. "I must have sounded terribly hard to you," she said.

Caleb's head lifted and his eyes caught hers. "No, you sounded terribly lost."

She knew his use of the word "lost" meant much more than just turning onto the wrong road. "I'm not lost now, Caleb. Thanks to you."

"I'm glad about that, Whitney. And thank you for the supper. It was very thoughtful and delicious."

His words made all the work she'd put into the meal worth it. Her smile glowed back at him.

"I wanted to do it, Caleb."

After the meal was over they took their coffee out on the front porch and sat down on the top step. Rebel was lying out on the cool grass of the yard. When the dog spotted Whitney and Caleb he jumped up on the porch and nudged his head between the two.

Caleb scratched the hound's ears, saying, "I'll bet you're ready for another hunt, aren't you, boy?"

"I should hope not!" Whitney said with fervor. "I spent all that day imagining you two dodging bullets."

"Listen at her, Rebel. She was worried about us."

"I suppose you like tracking down dangerous criminals?" she asked, her brows arched wryly.

With a complacent grin, Caleb leaned back on one elbow and crossed his boots at his ankles. Whitney looked down at him and longed to reach over and give his tousled curls a playful tug.

"Rebel and I like a good hunt every once in a while. It keeps things exciting." He glanced up at her as he sipped his coffee. "But aside from the hunts, someone like you would be bored to death living here."

"Why do you say that?"

"It's obvious. You're used to the city, the fast pace, the executive job, the bright lights and entertainment, the convenience. There's not much around here like that to fill a person's life."

His words puzzled her and she looked at him with a quizzical expression. "If I remember right, you're the same man who assured me that I would love it here. That the peace and quiet was good for a body."

He smiled crookedly at her choice of words. "Yeah, I did, didn't I? But just take this house for example," he said, looking back at the front door. "This house is old, my grandparents built it back in the early twenties. Down through the years it's been patched and remodeled, but it's nothing like what you're used to. It's serviceable, not beautiful."

"It's your home," Whitney said. "You should be proud of it. At least it's yours. The apartment I have is leased."

Caleb placed his empty cup out of the way. "Well, I saved for a long time to build a new house," he admitted. "A couple of years ago I decided I had enough money and even went so far as to talk to a building contractor. But when he came out and started talking about tearing the old place down I couldn't hardly stand it. I sent him away and forgot the whole idea." He sighed and looked up at Whitney. "Pearl called me a tightwad."

Whitney laughed softly, then leaned over and touched his shoulder. "I'd call you sentimental, Caleb Jones."

He smiled a little sheepishly. "Maybe so. I've lived here with my mama and daddy since I was ten years old. When I was twenty-one my daddy was transferred. He works for the state forestry division here in Louisiana," he explained. "If I hadn't stayed on, he was going to sell the place. It held too many memories for me to see it go to other hands."

"Family means a lot to you, doesn't it?"

He studied her face before answering. "Of course. Isn't family important to you?"

Whitney suddenly turned her head away from him. "It . . . it would be . . . if I had one," she murmured.

The starkness of her words cut into Caleb's heart. He shifted back to a sitting position as his eyes sought her face in the waning light.

His nearness was like a magnet to Whitney and she found herself drawn back to him.

He said, "You've spoken of your father. Your mother—"

"My father divorced my mother when I was very small," she cut in quickly. "There was a nasty custody battle, which my father ultimately won."

"You've always lived with him?"

Whitney nodded, drawing in a deep breath. "I was too young to really understand what went on in the trial, and for years I thought my mother didn't want me. During that time I clung to my father, frightened that he, too, would decide he didn't want a daughter. But as I grew older I got over all that," she said.

Caleb wondered if she really had gotten over it, or if she was just telling herself that she had. It had obviously been devastating for her when her father fired her from his advertising firm.

"What about your mother? Do you ever see her?"

Whitney gave a jerky nod. "Once in a while. Unfortunately a close bond never developed between us. And since she lives on the west coast now, there's a vast distance between us. It's rather hard to build a relationship when you have so little time to share with each other."

For long, thoughtful moments, Caleb's eyes roamed her face. There was a sadness in her eyes that he wanted to erase. She didn't deserve to be hurt, and he suddenly realized how much he would like to do for her, how much he wanted to give her and make her life happy.

"So for all these years, your father has been your family," he eventually murmured.

Whitney nodded again. "So now that he's fired me, I don't have much of anything where family is concerned."

"Whitney!" Caleb scolded softly. "The man fired you, he didn't disown you as a daughter. How could he? You're a woman any man would be proud to call his own."

Whitney's heart clung to his words. With everything inside her she wanted to believe him. But rejection in the past from those close to her made her too afraid to let herself believe him.

She reached over and touched his hand. "Maybe you wouldn't say that, Caleb, if you really knew me."

His other hand moved warmly over hers. "I do really know you, Whitney. I know that you're a bright, sensitive, caring woman. One that I'm getting damned attached to."

Whitney was completely surprised by his words, and her mouth fell open. Caleb leaned closer and promptly covered it with a kiss.

Whitney closed her eyes and reached out to him, wondering if he had any idea how much she needed him. How much she loved him.

Chapter Eleven

It was Caleb who eventually ended the kiss. Rising to his feet, he reached down and grasped both of Whitney's hands.

"Come on. Come with me to feed General," he invited.

At that moment Caleb could have led her anywhere and Whitney couldn't have refused him. She and Rebel went with him across the yard. Caleb curled his arm around her shoulders as they walked and Whitney smiled over at him.

The horse was already in the corral when they reached the barn. Caleb went to work measuring out the grain into the galvanized bucket. While Whitney poured it into the feed trough, Caleb filled the hay manger. When the tasks were finished, Caleb climbed up on the wooden fence and perched himself on the top rail. Whitney tossed him a sly glance, then hiked up her long skirt and followed his example.

The woods around them were deep and dark but filled with a multitude of night sounds. Frogs and insects sang and buzzed, while in the distance a whippoorwill called. Closer to them, General crunched into his oats and corn with healthy monotony. Every so often the horse swished his tail and stomped at a pestering insect.

Whitney settled herself atop the fence only inches from Caleb and breathed in deeply. "The first day I stayed here," she spoke, "I thought this place was quieter than a tomb. It made me want to scream just so I could hear something," she mused aloud. "But now I realize the woods aren't really quiet. There are all sorts of sounds out there to be heard. I'd just never taken the time to notice."

Her admission surprised him. He'd thought, and even hoped, that the place would become bearable for her. He'd never expected her to go as far as to appreciate it.

"Are you telling me you're actually beginning to like it here?" he asked.

His question made her realize just how much she was enjoying the quiet country life she'd had thrust upon her.

"Yes. But I suppose you find that difficult to believe," she replied.

Caleb's brows quirked with a faint frown. "Well, I keep remembering that first day you were here. I believe if I'd had a spare bicycle you'd have left on it," he said.

Whitney laughed softly. "I couldn't have pedaled all the way to Padre Island."

"I don't know about that. You had enough steam built up to go several hundred miles," he teased.

She laughed again, then looked over at him. Her expression grew serious as she met his eyes with hers. "I'm glad I didn't go. I'm glad you didn't let me go," she whispered.

He reached out and cupped the side of her face with his hand. Whitney wondered how his touch could feel so soft and tender when actually his palm was tough and callused. She liked to think it was because when he touched her, he touched her with his heart.

"I'm glad, too, Whitney. But I'm wondering how long it will be before the novelty of this place wears off."

"What do you mean?"

He grimaced, knowing his words weren't coming out the way he wanted them to. But when he was so near Whitney, his senses seemed to go haywire.

"I mean, if you stayed here for any length of time. You might like it now, but later on—" He stopped, shook his head, then dropped his hand from her cheek. "I guess I'm getting way ahead of myself, aren't I?"

Whitney looked at him hopefully. "I don't know. Are you?"

His fingers covered those of Whitney's that were holding on to the board fence. "We're very different people, Whitney. Our lives are completely opposite."

"You're not telling me anything I don't know, Caleb," she said.

"Well, I needed to hear myself say it out loud, anyway. Because I dread the time when you're going to leave. I don't want to think of this place without you here with me."

Was he telling her he loved her? she wondered wildly. An inexplicable feeling swelled in her breast. She found she had to swallow in order to utter a word.

"Maybe I won't want to leave," she said, barely aware of how hoarse and trembling her voice was.

"I don't think you've really thought about that, Whitney," he said after a moment. "You left your life hanging back in New York."

She shook her head fervently. "I didn't have a life in New York. I'm beginning to see that now."

Caleb grimaced once again and thrust his fingers through his hair. "Of course, you had a life. You were an important employee and—"

"Sure," she cut in dryly. "So important I was fired."

Caleb's fingers clamped over her shoulder. "And what about that, Whitney? Do you want to go back, work in advertising again?"

"I used to think so," she reluctantly admitted. "But that was before—" She took a deep breath and went on. "Before you became more important to me."

Caleb didn't say anything.

"There, I've said it. Have I shocked you?" Whitney asked.

His head shook slowly back and forth. "I'm trying to decide whether to kiss you, or to get down from here and run like hell."

She let out a shaky breath and leaned toward him. "I'd think kissing me would be much better. If you started running in the dark, you might trip over a snake, or possum, or whatever kind of creatures you have down here."

His mouth curved into a grin and in the next instant he was reaching out and drawing her into his arms.

"I think it's time my little old ladies started getting jealous," he murmured before moving his mouth onto hers.

His lips were hard and warm. As his mouth explored Whitney's face and throat, she forgot all about holding onto the fence. Her arms went around his neck with a fierce, possessive grip. She wanted this man more than she'd wanted anything in her life. When she was next to him, kissing him, she forgot all time and sense and reason.

When Caleb finally nestled her head against his shoulder, she was breathing rapidly and her body felt warm and languid.

"Is the fence moving, Caleb?"

He chuckled softly, "No, darlin', it's right where it was."

She pulled her head back and looked into his blue eyes. "You make me feel crazy, Caleb," she breathed the words. "Crazy and wonderful."

One corner of his mustache curved cockily upward. "And here I'd been thinking you were a cold-blooded Yankee."

Whitney reached up and pinched his jaw. He laughed again, then as he stroked her hair, his expression grew serious.

"Whitney, when I first asked you to stay I told myself it was because I'm such a good fellow and you needed help. Not counting the fact that you're damn pretty. Skinny, but pretty."

"Caleb—"

He shook his head, wanting her to let him go on. "I was attracted to you right from the start. But, hell, I guess you knew that, anyway."

"I like hearing it, anyway," she said, reaching up and pushing her fingers through the hair at his temple.

"I guess what I'm trying to say is that I've grown more than just attracted to you."

Whitney's eyes delved into his. "Why do I hear panic in your voice?"

His hands moved to her shoulders. "Whitney, that's not panic, that's caution," he said gently.

A crushed look came over her face, one that Caleb couldn't fail to miss. "I suppose that's because you...have doubts about me."

His head shook faintly as he searched for the right words. "I don't doubt you as a person, Whitney. I just doubt you fitting yourself into my life."

"Caleb, I just told you—"

His fingers touched her lips, stopping her words. "I know what you told me. Right now you're enjoying it here. But you've only been here for a few short days, Whitney. Spider says it will be another week before your car is finished. I want you to take that time to really think about things. About us. Will you do that for me?"

Whitney knew she could think until doomsday and her feelings wouldn't change. She loved this man, she wanted to spend her life with him. But he obviously wasn't ready to hear that from her, so she merely nodded at him.

"Yes. I will," she promised. To herself she promised that these next few days she would do everything in her power to show him how much she cared for him, how she could fit herself into his world. Maybe by the time her car was repaired, his doubts would be gone.

The next morning Whitney was awakened from a deep sleep by an insistent pounding.

She finally managed to crack her eyes open enough to see Caleb standing at the doorway to her bedroom. He was already fully dressed in jeans and his official khaki shirt.

"What is it?" she asked, groggily noticing it was still dark outside.

"I want you to come to work with me this morning," he said.

Whitney was instantly wide awake. "Go to work with you," she repeated. "Why?"

He grinned. "You'll see. Hurry. Breakfast is almost ready."

Breakfast! She'd meant to cook breakfast for him, or at least try to! Quickly she tossed back the covers and tied on her robe. After splashing her face and hands in the bathroom, she hurried out to the kitchen.

She found Caleb placing plates of bacon and eggs on the table. He said, "Be seated, Ms. Drake, and I'll have your coffee to you in just a moment."

Whitney tossed the tangled hair out of her eyes, looked at the cooked food, then over to him. "Caleb, I was going to cook your breakfast this morning."

He glanced at her over his shoulder as he filled two mugs with coffee. "That's all right, honey. You worked hard on supper last night. It was my turn."

"But Pearl had told me exactly how to do it!"

He started back to the table with the coffee. Motioning with his head for her to sit down, he said, "Whitney, it's nothing to get upset over. I'm not putting you down."

Whitney sat down across from him and took the coffee he handed her. Knowing it was steaming hot, she took a guarded sip. "It was just . . . something I wanted to do. I was always so busy back in New York. Not with domestic chores but with—"

"Your job," he finished for her as he sprinkled salt and pepper over his eggs.

"Yes," she reluctantly agreed, knowing it would never do to let him think she was missing her job. "But I just meant that I have a lot of energy and I need to focus it on something. And I think of cooking as an extension of my femininity."

This brought his face up and Whitney watched it crease with amusement. "An extension of your femininity? I just cooked our breakfast. What was I extending?"

She waved away his question and began to cut the fried egg on her plate. "The other day I heard a statistic about cooking that I found interesting. Even though most families consist of working wives, ninety-five percent of the wives still do all the cooking at home. It's just one of those things that go way back, I suppose. Like blue is for boys and pink is for girls."

"So now you think you want to be like the majority," he said, crunching into a piece of bacon.

She shrugged. "Well, I've tried the minority. I'm thinking it's time for a change."

Caleb studied her over the rim of his coffee cup. He didn't give a damn if she cooked or not. Loving a woman had nothing to do with the way she worked in the kitchen. There were more important things he was concerned about. Like her lost job and the rift between her and her father. But he wasn't going to say anything to her about it now. Last night he'd decided it would be better to take things slowly, to give her time to know what was in her mind and heart. He'd just have to wait it out.

"Did you pack a pair of jeans in your things?" he asked.

She looked at him curiously. "Yes, I think so. Why?"

He smiled at her. "Because you're going horseback riding today. Do you know how to ride?"

Whitney nodded. "I've ridden some. But that was a long time ago at summer camp."

"That's good enough. Riding is like kissing. Once you learn how to do it you never forget."

Whitney felt her cheeks fill with heat at his mention of kissing. It brought back last night at General's corral all too vividly. "Hmm. Well, I believe some people are more practiced," she told him.

The corners of his mouth tilted upward. "In riding, or kissing?"

"Both," she said, hurriedly reaching for her coffee mug while wishing he'd change the subject.

"Well, it all depends on what a person puts into it," he said lazily. "Don't you think?"

She met the glint in his eyes. "I think, Caleb Jones, that when your mother said you were handsome, she should have also added naughty."

"Naughty!" he said with exaggerated shock. "Now, Whitney, don't hurt my feelings so early this morning."

"I'm sorry," she said playfully.

"That's better," he said with a wink. "Now eat up. General's getting impatient and I'd hate for him to get out of sorts. He might throw us both off."

"Throw us! Caleb—" she began warningly.

"I'm only teasing, Whitney," he hastily assured her. "General's as tame as I am."

Whitney laughed and dug into her breakfast. She was looking forward to the day. Her heart felt light and happy, and she realized she'd never greeted her days back in the city with this state of mind. She'd always rushed anxiously to work, a thousand pressures weighing down on her mind. She'd been making money and a name for herself in the advertising business. But ultimately those things hadn't made her happy. She knew that now, because now she knew the difference between being driven and being happy. Caleb made her happy, more than she'd ever thought possible, and she couldn't bear to think of her life without him.

By the time Whitney had dressed in jeans, a pale peach blouse and pulled her hair back into a ponytail, Caleb had already hooked the horse trailer to the pickup and loaded General into it.

"Do I need to take my purse or anything?" Whitney asked when she joined him outside.

"Not really. I've brought a thermos of coffee, candy bars and a couple of slickers."

"Slickers?" Whitney automatically looked up at the sky. Or at least what patches she could see of it through the pine boughs above their heads. It seemed clear and blue. "Is it going to rain?"

"Thunderstorm, maybe," Caleb answered. "The air is still and humid. Feel it?"

"It's always still and humid. This morning doesn't feel any different to me."

"It is," he said, putting his hand against her back and urging her to climb into the truck. "But we're going to chance it anyway. Could be it'll decide not to storm at all."

When they reached the main highway, Caleb turned west. As they traveled, Whitney peeped through the gunrack on the back windshield. General had his brown nose stuck out a small window in the front of the horse trailer.

"General acts as though he likes to travel," she commented.

"General loves to travel. He likes a hunt just as much as Rebel."

"A hunt! Don't tell me we're going on one of those. I'm not ready to face a pack of criminals!"

Caleb let out a yelp of laughter. "Don't worry, Whitney, darlin', the most we might run into is a poacher or a moonshiner." He patted the pistol strapped to his hip. "And my trusty Colt will take care of that."

"Exactly where are we going?" she asked, wanting to forget the idea of running into danger.

"To the lake, but not quite."

"The lake?"

"Toledo Bend Reservoir. Part of it belongs to us Louisianans. The other part belongs to—" He grimaced and mouthed the word "Texas."

"We're going there, but not quite," she repeated. "What does that mean?"

He looked over at her and smiled. She was beautiful, even more so now that he'd come to know her.

"It means we're going to the north end to some of the creeks that channel into the lake. That's where the gators are."

"Gators?"

He nodded. "They're a protected species you know. I like to check on them from time to time."

Whitney looked out at the passing scenery thinking bemusedly that when she left New York she never dreamed she'd be checking alligators down in Louisiana. Her car accident had certainly taken her life on a different route. Whitney only hoped it wasn't a route that would eventually break her heart.

They traveled at least fifty miles or more before Caleb turned the pickup and horse trailer down a dusty, dirt road. It seemed to Whitney that they traveled for at least five bone-jarring miles before Caleb finally pulled to a stop.

He unloaded General and while she held the horse, he pulled the pickup completely off the road and onto a flat, grassy spot in order to be out of the way for passersby. Although Whitney couldn't imagine anyone going this far into the woods for any reason.

"Since I'm a Southern gentleman, I'm going to let you sit in the saddle," he told Whitney once he had their snacks and slickers tied behind the saddle.

He held the stirrup steady for her, and Whitney swung herself up. The next moment Caleb came up behind her and General started off in a slow walk. Whitney promptly handed the reins out to Caleb.

"You steer. I don't know where we're going anyway," she told him.

He reached around her waist and took the braided red nylon rein from her hand.

It caused his arm to curl around her waist. At the same time she felt his hard chest brush against her back. She'd forgotten the closeness involved in riding a horse double, and she wondered how she was going to focus her mind on anything but him.

Determinedly, she forced her eyes on the terrain around them and tried not to think of the scent and feel of him.

The land that stretched out in front of them was low and marshy. Whitney supposed it was typical Louisiana bayou. As General carried them along, his hooves made splashing, sucking noises in the mud and water. Spanish moss and purple wisteria draped the pines and cypress trees, making the woods seem canopied and closed off from the rest of the world.

"Will we see an alligator today?" Whitney asked.

"I imagine we'll see a few. They like to lay along the creek bank and sun themselves. They're lazy-type creatures, but they can move in the blink of an eye if they're agitated."

The steady rhythm of General's walk was lulling, like the gentle sway of a rocking chair. But the feel of Caleb's long, strong legs pressed up against the back of Whitney's was wildly distracting. She had to keep fighting the urge to turn her head and invite him to kiss her.

Chapter Twelve

For the next few minutes they traveled in silence. Eventually they came to a creek and Caleb guided General along the edge of the water.

"If the gators stay on the creek bank, aren't we asking to be eaten?" Whitney asked.

Caleb laughed softly and his left hand came up to knead her shoulder. Whitney closed her eyes and for a few special moments thought of nothing but his touch.

"Alligators don't attack people. They run from them."

"That's good news," Whitney said wryly.

The water seemed to be full of wildlife. Whitney spotted a group of mallard ducks and a bit farther on a flock of large black birds lined the branches of a dead cypress tree.

"Those are water turkeys," Caleb said. "Some people call them snakebirds because they swim beneath the surface of the water and their long necks look like snakes.

There's a big population of water turkeys living around the lake.''

They moved a few hundred more feet up the creek. Along the west edge of the bank a fallen log jutted partially out in the water.

"Look to your right about thirty yards ahead," he told her.

Squinting, Whitney's eyes traveled over the shallow creek. At first inspection she could see nothing out of the ordinary.

"Just to the left of the green bush at the water's edge," he clued. "It's long, scaly and has bulging eyes."

Its greenish-brown color blended with the surroundings, but Whitney finally spotted it. For long moments the alligator lay motionless on the muddy creek bank, seemingly oblivious to their presence. Just as Whitney was thinking how different it was to see animals in the wild instead of the zoo, the gator made a move and slid slowly into the water.

They traveled another mile and during that distance they spotted four more gators. Two of them were small, only about three or four feet in length. However, the other two were at least six feet long and heavily built.

When the ground became too marshy to continue, Caleb turned General around and headed back down the creek. Caleb searched out a spot of higher ground to dismount and let the horse rest. The day had grown smothering with heat and humidity. Whitney was not surprised to find her blouse wet and clinging to her.

After Caleb searched for snakes and found none, he allowed Whitney to sit on a half-rotted log. Sighing with relief at being out of the saddle, she stretched her legs out in front of her and fanned her face with her hand.

Caleb untied their things from the saddle and poured coffee. Squatting on his boot heels in front of Whitney, he handed the thermos cup to her, saying, "I should have brought something cold to drink. But there wasn't room for something with ice."

"This is lovely," Whitney said, glad for anything to quench her thirst.

"So, what do you think of your trip in a bayou?"

"Very interesting," she answered, her eyes on him. He'd pulled off his hat. His sandy hair lay flattened with sweat against his forehead and his khaki shirt was damp in the center of his chest. He was a strong, physical man. She was reminded of it every time she looked at him. "And very hot," she added.

"You probably wouldn't believe me if I told you that the lake itself is actually windy."

"Windy! There's not a drop of a breeze here." She handed him the cup. "You're right. I don't believe you."

"It's true, though. Sometime I'll take you out on the big water and let you see."

Sometime. Whitney hung on to the word. Did that mean he intended to ask her to stay? She wanted to ask him outright, but each time the words were on her tongue, she stopped herself.

Caleb held up three candy bars and she chose the one with chocolate and almonds.

After swallowing a bite, she said, "I must admit this place is as foreign to me as I suppose an advertising firm would be to you."

"I'd be lost," he admitted while unwrapping a piece of candy. "But I think I'd find it interesting. Advertising has a lot of influence on our lives, much more than most people realize. But I'm sure that you were aware of that long ago."

Once he'd finished tearing off the paper he crumpled it into a wad and stuffed it into his shirt pocket, then sat down on the log beside her.

"Very aware of it," Whitney answered. "That's why I never wanted to do a campaign for a product I didn't believe in. One of the arguments my father and I had was over a skin-care product. It was more or less ordinary cold cream, but this particular company wanted to push it as an anti-aging formula in order to sell it for a ridiculous price. We would have made big money on the account, but I felt we would have been cheating the public. My father has the attitude that if people are silly enough to be impressed by everything they see in advertising, then they only get what they deserve."

"That's very strange. It sounds like he's admitting that most advertisements are falsified."

Whitney shrugged. "Advertising is glossing over, creating an appealing impression. Whether it's done with romance, sex, humor, or whatever, it's just a way of presenting a product, not really informing the consumer."

He glanced over at her as he bit into his candy bar. "Is that what happened between you and your father?" he asked. "You disagreed on work?"

Whitney didn't resent Caleb's question. A week ago she would have. But she didn't now.

Sighing, she said, "My work seemed to be the basis of all our arguments. But I feel it goes much deeper than that." She shrugged with resignation and looked over at him. "I don't know what really happened between Father and me. I've always tried so hard to win his love, to gain his approval and pride. But it seemed like the more I tried the worse things became."

Sadness and confusion were threaded through her voice and it was all Caleb could do to keep from pulling her into his arms to comfort her. Yet Caleb knew that once she was in his arms the discussion about her father would be forgotten. And he didn't want that just now. He wanted to know everything about her, especially the parts that had saddened her life.

With slow, purposeful movements he ate the last of the candy bar, then poured another cup of coffee.

"Maybe that was the problem, Whitney. You tried too hard to make your father love you."

"What do you mean?"

He offered her the cup. She took a sip and handed it back to him.

"It means that you shouldn't have to work to make someone love you. Love is something that's given freely."

Frowning, she dug the toe of her canvas shoe into the damp, mulchy ground. "You don't understand, Caleb. My father doesn't give anything freely."

"What makes you think that? I would think your father loves you just for being his daughter."

"I know my father. I've lived around him all my twenty-eight years. With him you can't just *be*. In his eyes you have to do something before you can be something." She looked over at him and felt a lump begin to swell in her throat. Caleb was such a gentle, easygoing person. He probably couldn't imagine his family not loving him. "My mother was, and is still, very beautiful. She's intelligent and witty. On the whole, a nice person. But my father wasn't satisfied with her."

"Why do you think that was?" Caleb asked, hoping she would go on now that she'd opened up about her family.

Whitney shrugged, then reached up and scraped back a wisp of hair that had loosened from her ponytail. "I think it's because she wasn't ambitious. As far as the business world went," she added for explanation. "From what old friends of the family tell me, my mother was a dedicated wife and mother. But Father wanted her to be creative. She was content not to be."

Caleb shook his head in a disbelieving way. "So you've nearly worked yourself to death these past years in order to please him and gain his affection. My God, Whitney, can't you see how wrong that is?"

She had to look away from him as hot tears burned her eyes. "What is so wrong about wanting your father to love you?"

He reached over and clasped her hand in his. "Nothing is wrong in wanting your father's love. But you shouldn't have to work for it! From the way I see it, it seems as though everything you've done in life has been for him, not for yourself."

Is that really the way her life had been? she wondered. Her eyes filled with bewilderment as she looked back up at him. "I didn't think so. I thought I had been living for myself."

Caleb shook his head. "I don't think so."

Whitney suddenly bristled. "How would you know? You weren't there!"

"No," he agreed in an easy drawl, "but I'm here now. I'm seeing the end result of things."

Whitney opened her mouth to speak, but Caleb went on before she had the opportunity.

"And what about Edward? Were you going to marry him just because your father wanted you to?"

"I—" She stopped, unable to go on.

"Let me put it this way, Whitney. Were you going to marry Edward because you loved him?"

Glumly, Whitney shook her head. "No. I wasn't in love with Edward," she admitted, then looked at him a bit angrily. "Caleb, you're making me sound shallow and weak-minded. I'm not really that way."

He smiled and squeezed her hand. "I'm not trying to make you out to be weak-minded, Whitney, darlin'. I just want you to see what you've been doing to yourself. I want you to see that in order for others to love you, you first need to love yourself, be the person you want to be."

Deep down Whitney knew that what he was saying was true. But how did a person go about changing their directions after so many years? Besides, it scared her to think of just living for herself. What if she did? What if she even grew to love herself, but still no one else did? Especially Caleb? She couldn't bear to think of it.

"I suppose you're very fond of yourself?" she asked dryly.

He laughed deeply and squeezed her fingers. "Hell, Whitney, if I couldn't love me, who could?"

His laughter, the twinkle in his eye, plus his genuine concern for her lifted her heart. A smile crept slowly across her face.

Reaching over, she cupped her fingers against his jaw. "No one has ever made me feel the way you do, Caleb."

Caleb could not stop himself from leaning down and capturing her soft lips with his. Before the kiss barely began, Whitney's arms went up and around his neck. Caleb's hands spanned her slender waist. They instinctively drew closer, and the kiss grew longer.

Whitney had practically lost her breath by the time Caleb lifted his mouth.

"And I've never had a Yankee woman set a fire in me like you do," he murmured. "What do you suppose that means?"

She nuzzled her nose and mouth against his cheek. "It means you've never had a Yankee woman before."

Caleb wasn't expecting her teasing words. It was a moment before they sunk in, but when they did, his head fell back and he hooted with laughter.

Whitney smiled as she watched him, but then her expression grew serious. Her hands tightened on his neck as his laughter sobered and he looked back into her eyes.

She wanted to tell him how much she loved him. She wanted to tell him exactly how much she wanted to stay here in Louisiana and make her life with him. But she was so afraid to make that last final leap.

"Whitney," he murmured, "I—"

Whitney was instantly aware of the anxious look in his eyes.

"What is it?" she asked.

"I thought I heard thunder."

Whitney looked up through the tree limbs, listening keenly as she tried to see the sky overhead. "Thunder? Caleb, I really—"

She stopped speaking as she heard it, too. A low rumble was definitely sounding in the distance.

"I think we'd better load up and get back to the truck," he said quickly.

They had traveled close to fifteen minutes when the rain struck. Lightning bolted all around them, terrifying Whitney with its nearness. It seemed miraculous when, through the downpour, she saw the pickup and horse trailer.

She climbed into the cab while Caleb loaded the horse. When he slid in beside her, he took one look at her and burst out laughing. "That was a hell of a ride, wasn't it, darlin'?"

Something inside Whitney melted each time he called her "darlin'." The corners of her mouth tilted upward as she looked back at his wet face. "I must say the ride going up the creek was much more pleasant than the coming back down."

"Well, it never hurts to have a little excitement. It was going to be a disappointing trip if something hadn't happened. No poachers, no snakes, no moonshiners. Thank goodness that storm came along and saved things."

She unsnapped the yellow slicker and pulled it off her shoulders. "Caleb, you're crazy."

Lightning still bolted across the sky, the thunder was deafening. Involuntarily she inched closer to him.

Caleb watched her struggle to wipe the wet hair off her face.

"Do you know what you look like?" he asked.

Whitney frowned. "A drowned rat?"

"No. You look like that first night I found you in your car. You were wet and shaking then, too."

He put his arm around her and drew her up against him. Whitney nestled her head on his broad chest, thinking how much her life had changed since that night. Everything that had been in her heart had washed away and she'd been re-filled with need and love for this man.

"I may look the same. But I'm not the same." And she would prove it to him, she thought. In the time she had left with him she would make him see that she'd changed, that now he was the most important thing in her life.

Chapter Thirteen

The next week Whitney threw herself into Pearl's cooking lessons. Along with preparing meals, she scrubbed the house from top to bottom, did the laundry and struggled to learn how to iron Caleb's jeans and shirts.

Today her prime accomplishment had been to bake a pecan pie. Not quite the same as creating a car commercial, but to Whitney, infinitely more gratifying. Under Pearl's guidance the pastry had turned out very nice, she thought, and she was anxiously waiting for Caleb to come home to surprise him with his favorite dessert.

It was nearly dark when he did arrive. She and Rebel were sitting out on the porch when he drove up. Across the way, Pearl called out a greeting and he turned and waved at the old woman before moving on.

When he reached the porch, Whitney stood and latched her arm through his. He looked down at her smiling face, amazed at how natural it was for her to be here waiting for him. Once she was gone back to New York he couldn't imagine coming home and facing the old house alone.

"How was your day?" she asked.

"Very busy. I was unexpectedly called over to Hemphill, Texas, to testify in court."

"Oh? Anything serious?"

The two of them entered the house. He answered her question as he put away his hat and pistol. "A few months back we caught a couple of guys bringing stolen goods across the lake. Their trial just now came up on the docket." He sighed and raked his hands wearily through his hair. "The jury only deliberated fifteen minutes before returning a guilty verdict. It was pretty well cut and dried."

He looked unusually tired and she smiled at him, hoping to lift his spirits. "Well, that must have made you happy. To convict two Texans."

He shook his head. "No. I hate to discover anyone breaking the law, no matter where they're from."

"I was only teasing," she reasoned.

With a wry shake of his head, he gave her a halfhearted grin. He'd encouraged her time and again to loosen up, to tease and not take things too seriously. Now that she was, it made him feel even more down.

"I know you were, Whitney, darlin'," he said with a pat for her cheek. "Now I'd better go wash for supper."

Whitney nodded and he left the room. Thoughtfully she went to the kitchen and finished the last-minute details to her meal. Along with the pie, she'd prepared spaghetti, garlic bread and green salad. It was all on the table when Caleb entered the kitchen and took his seat.

He took in the meal, then lifted his eyes across to her. In spite of all the work she'd been doing the past few days, Caleb could see she had gained a small amount of weight.

Her cheeks weren't quite so thin and there was a natural rosiness to her complexion that had been absent when he'd first seen her. Tonight she was wearing a deep blue halter-top dress. She looked extremely lovely.

"I see you've been working hard again," he said, glancing away from her and down at the food.

She dismissed his words with a shrug. "Why do you always say I've been working hard? I must do something with myself."

"You've been bored?" he asked quickly.

Whitney frowned. "No. I've been learning, and I like that."

She passed him the bowl of spaghetti and he forked a portion onto his plate. Whitney could sense his changed mood. He was not the happy, lighthearted guy who always greeted her each evening.

"Is something wrong?" she asked.

He handed the bowl back to her. As she waited for him to answer, she twirled a portion of the pasta around the serving fork.

"Not really," he said. Then suddenly, with a sigh, he put his fork back down on the table. "I went by Spider's today."

Across the table Whitney met his eyes. She knew he was going to say the car was finally repaired. Her heart began to beat anxiously. Was he going to ask her to stay? To leave?

"Oh?"

"He has your Jaguar ready. It looks beautiful. Runs like a dream."

"That's . . . that's good. I fully intend to pay him extra. He's worked very hard on the car."

"That's very thoughtful of you, Whitney. But I doubt he'll accept it."

"If he doesn't, I'll drop it into a pocket on his baggy overalls while he's not looking. His wife will find it when she does the laundry."

A faint smile crossed Caleb's face and he reached once again for his fork.

Whitney swallowed as she felt the sting of tears at the back of her eyes. She didn't know why she was so close to crying. Her Jaguar was ready to drive. She should be happy. Instead she was miserable. The car's immobility had been the reason keeping her here with Caleb. Now there was no reason for her to stay. Unless it was love. But Caleb had never come out and told her he loved her. She was beginning to wonder if he considered the past two weeks merely a pleasant time between friends.

"So," she said on a deep breath, "when do I need to pick up the car?"

Caleb avoided her gaze as he ladled sauce over the pasta. "You don't have to. Spider is going to deliver it to you tomorrow morning. I thought you might want to get an early start back to New York."

Her heart plummeted painfully. It was all over, she thought dazedly. The closeness they'd shared the past two weeks had apparently meant nothing to him.

"Oh, I see." It was all she could manage to say. She felt tears in her eyes but she determinedly blinked them back. She could no longer be that soft-hearted woman. She would have to go back to her tough armor, back to New York, back to a life alone.

Whitney spent the remainder of the meal merely pushing the food around her plate. When it came time to serve Caleb the pie she'd been so proud of, she could barely stand to look at it.

"If you'll excuse me, Caleb. I'm just not hungry," she told him, quickly scraping back her chair and rising to her feet.

"Whitney?"

She didn't stay to answer his question. Hurrying out of the kitchen, she went straight to her room.

Glancing around at the small space she'd become so used to, she decided she should busy herself with packing her things. But instead of pulling out her suitcase, she simply sank down on the bed and closed her eyes.

She wasn't aware of how long she sat there or when Caleb entered the room.

He touched her shoulder and she jumped with a start.

"I didn't mean to frighten you," he apologized.

Whitney didn't look at him. Shaking her head, she said, "I didn't hear you. How did the pie taste?"

"I don't know. I didn't eat it."

This brought her face up to his. "Why not?"

He eased down beside her and Whitney felt herself quivering at his closeness. She loved him so much. Didn't he realize that by now? Or maybe he did realize it but he just couldn't return the same feeling.

"I wanted you to eat a piece of it with me. That's why."

"I told you. I'm not hungry."

"Then I'm not, either," he said.

"I took great pains with the pie. I wanted to surprise you," she told him in a small voice.

"You did."

She turned her eyes on him. The dismal look on his face matched the pain in her heart.

"What's wrong, Caleb?" she whispered.

"I feel terrible," he said.

She swallowed as a lump formed in her throat. Yet swallowing did no good. She couldn't stop herself from burying her face against his chest. "Oh, Caleb," she sobbed. "I don't want to leave you. Don't you know that by now?"

His arms came around her, his hand gently stroked her black hair. "I don't really want you to leave, either, Whitney. But I've thought about this over and over. I think it's for the best."

Sniffing, she drew her head back and looked into his eyes. "Why? Caleb, I love you. You told me to take these past few days to think about me, you and my life, remember?"

He nodded gravely and she went on. "Well, I have. It's all I have thought about. And I know I want to stay here with you."

His hand came up to cup her cheek as he leaned forward and kissed her forehead. "I love you, too, my darlin'. And sending you back to New York is probably the hardest thing I've ever had to do."

He loved her! For a moment it was all her mind could register.

"I don't understand, Caleb. If you love me—"

His hand dropped from her face and gently slid up and down her forearm. "That's why I have to send you back, because I do love you. If you remember, you left your life hanging back there. I don't want us to start off that way."

"That life is gone," she argued.

He shook his head. "You need to be sure of that, Whitney. Right now you think it is, but is that how you'd feel two weeks from now, two months from now? I want us to be married, Whitney. I want us to have children. That's a big commitment. And Manhattan is as opposite of this place as you can possibly get. You need to be sure this is the life you want."

Her hands reached up to frame his face. The fact that he loved her and wanted to marry her filled her heart with such joy.

"It's all I'll ever want."

His hands tightened around her waist. "I hope that's true, Whitney. With all my heart I hope you'll come back in two weeks and tell me you want to marry me. But I also want to know that you're certain about it. That you won't miss your work and the city life."

"It won't take me two weeks to decide that," she countered.

"I want you to take them, anyway."

"What makes you think I don't know my own mind? Why won't you believe I've changed? Your sending me back is only going to hurt me."

He reached up and pulled her hands from his face to hold them both clasped between his. "Because I can see that you haven't yet learned that love is something that's given, not gained. The past days you've worked like a Trojan, doing things for me to please me. Don't you understand, Whitney? I don't care if you can cook or sew or stand on your head. I love you just for you, not because of the things you can do. You made that mistake with your father."

Whitney frowned at him. "He's out of my life now."

"That's where you're wrong. And that's another reason why you have to go back."

"My father? Why should I want to go back for his sake?" she asked hoarsely.

"Because you love him," Caleb said simply.

Whitney's eyes dropped. "Yes. But he doesn't love me."

"I think you're wrong about that. But either way I think you should be able to tell him, 'Here I am. Love me the way I am, or don't love me at all.'"

"This is really important to you, isn't it?" she asked, surprised that it should matter so much to him.

One corner of his mouth lifted. "I might be a bachelor, but family is important to me. And I happen to want you happy. Once you get to New York, you'll understand all the things I've been saying to you."

Groaning, Whitney leaned forward and lay her cheek against his shoulder. "Once I get to New York I won't see anything but you."

His hand stroked her hair as he pressed his jaw against the top of her head. "Once you get to New York you may decide you don't want anything else to do with Louisiana, or game rangers."

"I'll always want this game ranger," she said, the ferocity of her voice muffled by his shirt.

Caleb closed his eyes and held her tightly to him. New York seemed like a world away, and he wondered if he'd ever get to hold her again.

Whitney's drive back to New York took four tiring, uneventful days. She found the city warm with late spring and the trees covered with green leaves.

The first day back she spent unpacking and resting from the long drive. The second day she felt restless and confined behind the walls of her apartment. She found herself longing to hear the birds, to open the window and smell the pines.

Impulsively she dressed in jeans and went down to Central Park. But as she strolled along, all she could think of was Caleb. She wondered how he was and what he'd been doing. She wondered if he'd gone back to eating sardines and crackers for supper, or if Pearl had been going over and cooking for him.

Whitney missed the cooking. She'd tried making a few things for herself since she'd been back, but it just hadn't seemed the same. Not without the person you loved to share it with.

The park was full of joggers and people out playing in the warm weather. Many had their pets with them. She saw several dogs, but none resembling a hound like Rebel. The cats reminded her of Chester and Bernice, and even the policeman's horse made her think of General.

Finally she gave up on trying not to think about Caleb or anything connected to him and went back to her apartment.

On the third morning she decided the only thing left to do was go to the firm and see her father. She knew she couldn't go back to Louisiana unless she did. Caleb wouldn't have it any other way. And deep down Whitney wanted things to be resolved between her and her father. Or at least if they couldn't be resolved, she wanted Caleb to know that she'd tried.

She dressed in a beige linen suit with a straight skirt and double-breasted jacket. In the old days she would have pulled her hair into a no-nonsense twist at the back of her head, but today she left it loose and waving casually about her face.

The advertising offices were located in busy midtown Manhattan. Rather than risk ruining Spider's beautiful paint job on her Jaguar, she took a cab.

As Whitney entered the double glass doors she saw the same receptionist sitting behind the front desk.

"Hello Mary Anne," she said with a bright smile.

"Ms. Drake? I—it's good to see you again."

The young blonde was obviously shocked at seeing her there.

"It's good to see you, too, Mary Ann. Would you happen to know if my father is in?"

Her expression rather sheepish, the receptionist shook her head. She, like everyone else in the offices, had heard about Mortimer Drake firing his daughter.

"I'm afraid not, Ms. Drake. He's out on the west coast at some sort of conference."

Whitney was disappointed. She'd wanted to get this meeting over with for more than one reason. But there was nothing she could do about it now.

"I see. Well, I guess I'll just say hello to some people. Take care, Mary Anne."

The receptionist smiled and nodded. Whitney walked away from the desk and started down a wide corridor.

"Oh, Ms. Drake?" Mary Anne called.

Whitney looked over her shoulder to see the young blond-headed woman nervously chewing on her lip. "I—I just thought I should tell you that Mr. Drake, er, your father has already hired someone in your place."

Whitney smiled resignedly. "I had already expected as much," she assured the woman. "Don't worry about it."

Mary Anne nodded with relief and Whitney continued on down the hall. The red carpet and oak paneling was the same as it had been for the past several years, but this was the first time Whitney had really taken time to notice her surroundings.

She passed several office doors then stopped at a wide wooden one to her left. The name on the brass plate used to be hers. Now it read Edith Carlson. Well, she thought dryly, at least he hadn't replace her with a man.

Moving on down the corridor she turned to her right, then entered another door. It was the art-design room, and presently in as much chaos as it had always been. A dark-headed man with his hair pulled back into a ponytail lifted his head to see Whitney first. His eyes widened in disbelief, making a smile spread across Whitney's face.

"You're not seeing a ghost, Danny. It is really me."

He hurried toward her. "Whitney, I never thought I'd see you here again. Are you coming back to the firm?"

Whitney shook her head. "No. I came by to see Father. But Mary Anne tells me he's out."

"Yeah, that's right," he said. "God, where have you been? Is this really you, Whitney? You seem so different."

Whitney laughed with a freedom that came from deep within her. As she looked around the room where she'd spent so many harrowing hours in the past, she was keenly aware that nothing in it interested her. She knew with unshakable certainty that being an executive in advertising was not what she wanted for herself. It never really had been, but it had taken Caleb's love to make her see it.

She smiled at Danny. "This is the real me, Danny."

"But you're so glowing and relaxed! What did this to you? I mean, can I have a shot of it?"

She laughed and started toward the door. "Just try hunting alligators. I did," she tossed over her shoulder.

Three days later Whitney sat in her apartment, staring out the window at the steady rain falling over the city. It was a quiet spring rain, nothing like the torrential storm that had battered her and Caleb in the bayou.

Still, the rain made her even more pensive, and several times she thought of calling Caleb. Yet each time she reached for the phone she stopped herself. She knew if she heard his voice she'd get all weepy, which would upset him, and make her even more miserable. Besides, she still hadn't seen her father and she knew that would be the first thing Caleb would question her about.

A knock at the door brought Whitney out of her reverie.

"I'll get it," Mrs. Devlin, her housekeeper, called from the kitchen.

"Oh, do come in," Whitney could hear her saying to the caller. "Yes, she is in. Let me take your coat and umbrella."

Whitney started to rise from the couch just as her father appeared in the room. The sight of him shocked her. He'd rarely taken the time in the past to visit her, making him the last person she expected to see walk into the room.

"Hello, Whitney. May I sit down?"

So formal, she thought. Pearl treated her with more familiarity than her own father. "Of course," she said, scooting down to the end of the couch to make room for him.

"Would you like a drink?" she asked once he was settled.

"It's early in the evening but a Scotch would be nice."

Whitney got to her feet to go fix the drinks, but at that moment Mrs. Devlin appeared in the room.

"I'll get them, Ms. Drake," she assured Whitney.

"Scotch and ice for my father, Mrs. Devlin, and a seltzer water for me, please."

The housekeeper moved away to the bar and Mortimer Drake turned toward his daughter. "I was told you came by the office a few days ago."

She was only a couple of cushions away from him, but still he felt so distant. It was a very sad thought for Whitney. "Yes, I did."

"For a certain reason?"

She looked at him, taking in his iron-gray hair, dark eyes and deeply lined face. For the first time she looked at him as a man instead of as her father or her boss. He was human and flawed, just like everyone else. Why hadn't she realized that long ago?

"Just to say hello and to let you know I was back in the city."

Mrs. Devlin arrived with the drinks. Mortimer took his and tossed half of it down before he spoke. "I thought you might have wanted your job back."

Whitney laughed because she could laugh now. Caleb had taught her how. "I have no desire for my job back."

This brought her father's eyebrows to twin peaks. "I don't understand. When you left here you were hellbent about it."

Smiling faintly, she crossed her legs and took a sip of her seltzer water. "I'm a different woman now than I was then."

"You were very angry," he said.

"Very angry and very hurt," Whitney agreed. "And I guess a part of me is still hurt because my own father sacked me."

Grimacing, he said, "It wasn't something I wanted to do."

Whitney watched her father as he rose from the couch and crossed over to the bar to refill his glass. Whitney was amazed at how things had turned around so completely. Her father was now the nervous one.

"Then why did you?" she asked.

"We didn't get along."

"That's nothing new. You don't get along with half of your employees."

He snorted and came back to take his seat on the couch. "I tried to tell you, Whitney. I didn't like what the job was doing to you, the kind of woman it was making you. But each time I tried, you took it offensively."

"It's not very pleasant having someone tell you you've turned into a shrew," she reasoned, "but that doesn't matter anymore. I have something else to talk about."

"Oh? You've been hired by another firm?"

She shook her head. "While I've been away I met a man."

Whitney was astonished to see a pleased look on his face. "What sort of man?"

She laughed under her breath, because when her thoughts went to Caleb they always lifted her heart.

"He's a state game ranger in Louisiana."

"That's interesting. Did you get to know him well?"

"Very well. I've fallen in love with him," she said seriously.

"And him?" Mortimer questioned.

"He loves me, also."

"Then why are you here in New York instead of with him?"

That was the last thing she'd expected her father to say. She'd been expecting all sorts of cross-examination about Caleb.

"To be honest, I'm here because he sent me back. He wanted me to have time to think things through—and to see you again. He wanted me to tell you something."

Mortimer looked curiously at his daughter. "What was it?"

Clasping her hands in her lap, she lifted her chin and looked her father in the eye. "Here I am, Father. Love me the way I am, or not at all. Either way, I have to be my own person."

For long moments he looked at her, and as he did, his eyes softened with understanding. Then, slowly, he leaned toward her and enfolded her in his arms. "Whitney, you're my daughter. I'll always love you. Haven't you known that?'' he asked, his voice husky with affection.

Tears oozed from beneath Whitney's closed eyelids. "Caleb said that you loved me. I was afraid to believe him."

Smiling, Mortimer put her from him. "Then he's obviously a smart man."

Whitney reached up and wiped away her tears. "He is a smart man, Father. A wonderful man. He's made me realize that being an executive in the business world is not me."

"I knew that long ago, Whitney. That's why I fired you. Not to hurt you, but to help you. You were allowing your job to alienate you from friends and loved ones, from life even."

Shaking her head she said, "I thought my being in the business was what you wanted, expected. I didn't want to disappoint you. You divorced Mother—"

Regret washed over the older man's face. "Because I devoted too much time to achieving success instead of my wife, she looked to someone else for the affection I failed to give her. I didn't want to make that same mistake with you, Whitney. I didn't want you to make the same mistake I did. I want you to be happy."

Whitney felt a great relief at her father's words, but she also felt a sense of sad loss for her parents, for herself. So many mistakes and misunderstandings had been made. But now the future would be better. Caleb had made it that way.

"All these years I've tried so hard to be what I thought you wanted me to be. I tried to be as unlike Mother as I could possibly be. But ironically, the past days I spent in Louisiana, I discovered I'm very much like her. I want a husband and family more than anything in my life."

Mortimer smiled with pride at his daughter. "You are very much like her, Whitney, and I love you. I haven't met your Caleb yet. But I already know one thing—I'm very glad you found him."

There were tears in Whitney's eyes as she smiled at her father. But they were tears of a happiness too great to contain. "I am too, Father. Very glad."

Chapter Fourteen

The hot Louisiana sun beat down on Whitney's arms and shoulders. Earlier in the day she'd put the top down on the car. Already she was becoming lobster red, but she didn't care. The Southern heat felt wonderful as it seeped into her skin and her bones. So did the knowledge that she was finally going home.

She turned her Jaguar down the dirt lane leading to Caleb's house. This time she wasn't lost in navigation—or heart. She knew exactly where she was going and her spirits soared high as she drew closer and closer.

When she pulled the car to a stop in front of the house, she found Caleb's pickup parked beneath its usual pine tree. Rebel was lying in the yard. The dog jumped to his feet and barked at the strange vehicle, but as soon as Whitney called his name, he instantly recognized her voice and began to whine and twist his body with excitement.

She hurriedly climbed out of the car and hugged the dog to her, then rising, she looked toward the house. Caleb apparently hadn't heard her drive up. He wasn't any-where in sight.

Whitney quickly climbed the steps and crossed the porch, calling his name as she went.

"Caleb? Are you here?"

She heard footsteps as she opened the screen door. Then suddenly he appeared from the direction of the bed-rooms. He went stock-still as he spotted her.

"Whitney!"

She ran to him, flinging herself against him with a happy sob. He held her so tightly she could scarcely breathe, and she clung to him, laughing and crying at the same time.

"Oh, darlin'," he groaned. "it's been almost three weeks. I've been calling your apartment and not getting an answer."

"I know. I know," she hastily interrupted, leaning her head back so that she could look up at his dear, familiar face. "It took me a while to get a few business details taken care of. Like my apartment and banking, but for the past few days I've been on the road, on my way back to you."

Groaning again, he pulled her head back against his chest and held her tightly for long moments.

"I was beginning to think you'd decided to stay in New York," he said with gruff emotion. "I was beginning to think I'd never see you again. I was beginning to think I was the fool of all fools for letting you go back."

Whitney laughed softly, sexily, as she pushed away from him. "Not a chance, Mr. Jones. You're stuck with me now."

He caught her hands with his as he looked deep into her eyes. "Are you sure, Whitney? I love you so much that I want you here with me more than anything. But I also want you to be happy. I want us to be happy."

Her fingers squeezed his as she smiled back at him. "You were right sending me back to New York, Caleb. It made me see things very clearly. Everything about my old life looked sterile and meaningless without you. My apartment, my job—"

"And your father? What about him?"

Her eyes blinked as tears gathered. "Oh, Caleb, he said the most wonderful thing to me. He said I was very much like my mother, and that he loved me."

Caleb grinned as he drew her back into his arms. "Of course, he does. You're a special woman, Whitney. It's why we both love you."

She slanted him a coy glance from beneath her black lashes. "If that's the case, then why are you being so slow about showing me?"

Laughter gurgled in his throat. "Whitney, darlin', you know how it is down here in the South. Slow and ea—"

The rest of his words were smothered as Whitney leaned up on tiptoe and covered his mouth with hers.

After that it was long, long minutes before there was any more conversation. But eventually Caleb gathered Whitney by the hand and led her into his bedroom.

"I want to show you what I was doing before you drove up," he told her.

Whitney looked around the room. Clothes were piled here and there. Some were already folded into a suitcase, others lay waiting to follow.

"What is this?" she asked, completely confused. "You were going somewhere?"

"To New York. To get you."

Her brown eyes met his blue ones and she felt her heart burgeon with love and happiness. This man was everything to her. "You love me that much?"

"I love you that much."

She reached over and dumped the suitcase of clothes back onto the bed. Then sliding her arms around his waist, she said, "And I love you that much. You'll never have to go anywhere for me. I'll always be right here—in your arms."

Caleb tilted her face up and gave her a long, thorough kiss. Then laughing softly, he drawled, "Just wait till all my little old ladies hear about this."

Epilogue

A little over two years later, Whitney and Caleb stood side by side out in the yard, looking up at the new rafters and gable the carpenters were adding onto the east side of the house.

"I don't know, Whitney," Caleb was saying. "What in the world would we do with a fireplace? You know it rarely ever gets to thirty degrees down here."

"Well, it wouldn't have to be thirty degrees to build a fire," she reasoned. "We could build one if it got to forty, couldn't we?"

Caleb looked down at her and laughed. Whitney made a playful face up at him.

His eyes softened and his arm came around her shoulders. "Do you really want one that badly?"

She nodded, then gave him a sexy look. "Just think how nice it would be darling. With nothing but the firelight, me and you, and a glass of wine. I've always dreamed of making love to you in front of a fireplace."

His brows lifted, then leaning his head close to hers, he grinned cockily. "Oh, really? Well, I've dreamed of making love to you in the kitchen, the living room, the bathroom, the closet, the floor, the pickup, the barn—" He kept going, but Whitney's laughter drowned out his list.

"What's all the laughter about?"

Both of them looked up to see Pearl and Whitney's father, who was carrying his six-month-old granddaughter, Gina. It was her father's third visit since Whitney had married Caleb and borne a daughter. This time Mortimer was on a short vacation and planned to stay three days. Whitney was enjoying having him around very much. Especially when she saw how much he loved being with his granddaughter.

"Caleb and I were just discussing the fireplace."

"What's the verdict?" he asked. The dark-haired girl in his arms whined and reached for her mother. Whitney took her with the natural ease that came with the loving bond between mother and child.

Caleb answered, "This house has been here over sixty-five years without a fireplace, but we've decided we just can't live without one." He gave Whitney a sly wink.

"You know," Mortimer said, "five years ago if someone had told me Whitney would be living in a place like this and loving it, I would have accused them of insanity."

All of them laughed and Pearl commented, "When Caleb first brought Whitney home, she was as nervous as a cat on a hot roof. But she came around."

She'd come around all right, Whitney silently mused. The past years with Caleb had been even more wonderful than she'd imagined. His love contented her, excited her, filled her with constant joy.

Before she'd met Caleb she'd been a lonely woman hiding behind her job as an executive. She'd believed that drive and determination would gain her love and happiness. But Caleb had made her realize that forcing herself to be a tough-minded business woman was only making her and those around her miserable. He'd taught her that love was something given freely, not something to be earned. Now she was happier than she'd ever dreamed possible. Yes, she thought contentedly, Caleb's southern touch had brought her around all right.

*   *   *   *   *

COMING NEXT MONTH

#724 CIMARRON KNIGHT—Pepper Adams
A Diamond Jubilee Book!
Single mom Noelle Chandler thought she didn't need a knight in
shining armor. Then sexy rancher Brody Sawyer rode into her life.
This is Book #1 of the *Cimarron Stories.*

#725 FEARLESS FATHER—Terry Essig
Absent-minded Jay Gand fearlessly tackled a temporary job of
parenting. After all, how hard could it be? Then he found out, and
without neighbor Catherine Escabito he would never have survived!

#726 FAITH, HOPE AND LOVE—Geeta Kingsley
Luke Summers's ardent pursuit of romance-shy Rachel Carstairs was
met by cool indifference. But Luke was determined to fill the lovely
loner's heart with faith, hope . . . and his love.

#727 A SEASON FOR HOMECOMING—Laurie Paige
Book I of HOMEWARD BOUND DUO
Their ill-fated love had sent Lainie Alder away from Devlin Garrick—
and her home—years ago. Now, Dev needed her back. Would her
homecoming fulfill broken promises of the past?

#728 FAMILY MAN—Arlene James
Weston Caudell's love for his estranged nephew warmed wary Joy
Morrow, but would the handsome businessman leave as quickly as
he'd come—with her beloved charge . . . and her heart?

#729 THE SEDUCTION OF ANNA—Brittany Young
Dynamic country doctor Esteban Alvarado set his sights on Anna
Bennett, but her well-ordered life required she resist him. Yet Anna
hadn't counted on Esteban's slow, sweet seduction. . . .

AVAILABLE THIS MONTH:

#718 SECOND TIME LUCKY
Victoria Glenn

#719 THE NESTING INSTINCT
Elizabeth August

#720 MOUNTAIN LAUREL
Donna Clayton

#721 SASSAFRAS STREET
Susan Kalmes

#722 IN THE FAMILY WAY
Melodie Adams

#723 THAT SOUTHERN TOUCH
Stella Bagwell

DIAMOND JUBILEE CELEBRATION!

It's the Silhouette Books tenth anniversary, and what better way to celebrate than to toast *you*, our readers, for making it all possible. Each month in 1990 we'll present you with a DIAMOND JUBILEE Silhouette Romance written by an all-time favorite author! Saying thanks has never been so romantic...

The merry month of May will bring you SECOND TIME LUCKY by Victoria Glenn. And in June, the first volume of Pepper Adams's exciting trilogy Cimarron Stories will be available—CIMARRON KNIGHT. July sizzles with BORROWED BABY by Marie Ferrarella. Suzanne Carey, Lucy Gordon, Annette Broadrick and many more have special gifts of love waiting for you with their DIAMOND JUBILEE Romances.

If you missed any of the DIAMOND JUBILEE Silhouette Romances, order them by sending your name, address, zip or postal code, along with a check or money order for $2.25 for each book ordered, plus 75¢ for postage and handling, payable to Silhouette Reader Service to:

In the U.S.	In Canada
901 Fuhrmann Blvd.	P.O. Box 609
P.O. Box 1396	Fort Erie, Ontario
Buffalo, NY 14269-1396	L2A 5X3

Please specify book title(s) with your order.

January	ETHAN by Diana Palmer (#694)
February	THE AMBASSADOR'S DAUGHTER by Brittany Young (#700)
March	NEVER ON SUNDAE by Rita Rainville (#706)
April	HARVEY'S MISSING by Peggy Webb (#712)

SRJUB-1A

A TRILOGY BY PEPPER ADAMS

Pepper Adams is back and spicier than ever with three tender, heartwarming tales, set on the plains of Oklahoma.

CIMARRON KNIGHT...coming in June

Rugged rancher and dyed-in-the-wool bachelor Brody Sawyer meets his match in determined Noelle Chandler and her adorable twin boys!

CIMARRON GLORY...coming in August

With a stubborn streak as strong as her foster brother Brody's, Glory Roberts has her heart set on lassoing handsome loner Ross Forbes...and uncovering his mysterious past....

CIMARRON REBEL...coming in October

Brody's brother Riley is a handsome rebel with a cause! And he doesn't mind getting roped into marrying Darcy Durant—in name only—to gain custody of two heartbroken kids.

Don't miss CIMARRON KNIGHT, CIMARRON GLORY and CIMARRON REBEL—three special stories that'll win your heart...coming soon from Silhouette Romance!